S0-BRE-578

Clenching his jaw, Devon yanked Todd with all his might. The belt loop broke, and he and Todd tumbled to the ground just as the barrier broke completely, sending the Jeep smashing into the rocks hundreds of feet below.

Sprawled across the road with Todd's dead-weight on top of him, Devon struggled to catch his breath as his adrenaline-induced strength disappeared. He rested on the blacktop a few seconds, then eased himself from beneath Todd, carefully laying Todd's head on the road.

"Todd!" Elizabeth cried, throwing herself over his motionless body.

Devon gently reached down and pulled Elizabeth away. "It's best not to move him or touch him right now," he told her. "He's been pretty badly shaken."

"Oh, Devon," Elizabeth cried, burying her head in his shoulder.

Devon held her close to him. "It'll be all right, Liz," he comforted her as they waited for an ambulance. But Devon wondered how truthful he was being. Todd had been seriously hurt. He'd suffered a severe blow to his skull and maybe internal injuries they didn't know about.

Elizabeth lifted her head, desperately searching Devon's eyes. "Todd can't die," she told him. "I can't live without him."

Visit the Official Sweet Valley Web Site on the Internet at:

http://www.sweetvalley.com

PLEASE
FORGIVE ME

Written by
Kate William

Created by
FRANCINE PASCAL

BANTAM BOOKS
NEW YORK · TORONTO · LONDON · SYDNEY · AUCKLAND

RL 6, age 12 and up

PLEASE FORGIVE ME
A Bantam Book / May 1998

Sweet Valley High® is a registered trademark of Francine Pascal.
Conceived by Francine Pascal.
Produced by Daniel Weiss Associates, Inc.
33 West 17th Street
New York, NY 10011.
Cover photography by Michael Segal.

All rights reserved.
Copyright © 1998 by Francine Pascal.
Cover art copyright © 1998 by Daniel Weiss Associates, Inc.
No part of this book may be reproduced or transmitted
in any form or by any means, electronic or mechanical,
including photocopying, recording, or by any information
storage and retrieval system, without permission in
writing from the publisher.
For information address: Bantam Books.

If you purchased this book without a cover you should be aware
that this book is stolen property. It was reported as "unsold and
destroyed" to the publisher and neither the author nor the publisher
has received any payment for this "stripped book."

ISBN: 0-553-49230-6

Published simultaneously in the United States and Canada

Bantam Books are published by Bantam Books, a division of Bantam
Doubleday Dell Publishing Group, Inc. Its trademark, consisting of the
words "Bantam Books" and the portrayal of a rooster, is Registered in U.S.
Patent and Trademark Office and in other countries. Marca Registrada.
Bantam Books, 1540 Broadway, New York, New York 10036.

PRINTED IN THE UNITED STATES OF AMERICA

OPM   0 9 8 7 6 5 4 3 2 1

To Allison Dale Stone

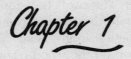

Chapter 1

Sixteen-year-old Elizabeth Wakefield paced the oak floor of her living room, an angry frown wrinkling her forehead. It was Sunday evening. Outside, Todd Wilkins—Elizabeth's longtime boyfriend until a little over a week ago—was pounding on the front door, begging her to listen.

Elizabeth blocked her ears and paced even harder. As she passed the walnut coffee table her eyes fell on an unopened box of imported Belgian chocolates and a bouquet of yellow roses that Todd had sent her. The roses were called Yellow Sunblaze because of the brilliant pink that edged their lemon yellow petals. They were some of Elizabeth's favorite flowers, but now she couldn't bear to look at them. Not after what had happened that afternoon at the Dairi Burger between Todd and Devon Whitelaw.

Elizabeth covered her ears more tightly as Todd continued to beg her to listen from the other side of the door. The cards he'd sent her filled the coffee table—cute, funny, and romantic cards, all begging Elizabeth's forgiveness. There were so many, they obscured the wood-framed portraits of her family and pieces of lopsided pottery that her mother had saved from Elizabeth, Jessica, and Steven's grade-school days. A few of Todd's cards had been opened, but most—like the chocolates—remained sealed.

Mixed in with Todd's gifts were presents from Devon Whitelaw. There was a bottle of liquid the blue-green color of Elizabeth's eyes that Devon had made in chem lab, a heart-shaped wreath composed of pink tea roses and baby's breath, and a leather-bound edition of Elizabeth Barrett Browning's poems, inscribed, *These words barely touch the surface of my feelings for you.* Elizabeth would have loved these things once, but now they just heightened the confusion and hurt pulsing through her veins. *The two of them are even bigger idiots than I thought if they think they can buy my love,* she told herself angrily.

"Liz, please! Just let me explain!" Todd yelled from the other side of the door.

"Leave me alone!" Elizabeth yelled back. "Just get out of my life!" The pounding stopped, and a moment later she heard the sound of Todd's BMW screeching out of the driveway. *Good,* she thought.

She didn't want to hear explanations. Todd would never be able to explain what had happened at the Dairi Burger—would never be able to justify how the two boys she cared for most in the world had ended up fighting like wild animals in the name of love.

Angry tears welled in her eyes as she recalled last week, when everything had started. It had all happened so innocently. A harmless flirtation with Devon in chem lab that had grown into a full-blown love affair. She had never meant to hurt Todd, but she hadn't been able to control her heart.

When her twin sister, Jessica, had found out about Elizabeth and Devon, she'd freaked. Jessica had wanted Devon for herself and had seen an opportunity to get revenge on Elizabeth by setting up Courtney Kane with Todd. Courtney—tall and curvaceous, with shiny mahogany hair and eyes the color of smoke—was one of the biggest snobs Elizabeth had ever met. A student at posh Lovett Academy, Courtney had tried to steal Todd from Elizabeth before and had been only too happy to try to steal him again.

At first Elizabeth had felt a twinge of jealousy when she learned about Todd and Courtney. But then she had reasoned that if she was seeing Devon, Todd should be able to see someone too. When she had asked Todd to meet her at the Dairi Burger this afternoon, it had been to tell him how happy she was that he'd found someone. She had wanted to tell Todd it was OK for him to give Courtney the beautiful silver ring he'd bought for the anniversary of Elizabeth's first published story.

Elizabeth grimaced as she recalled the hopeful, pained look in Todd's eyes when he'd given her the ring. It had been a lovely gesture. Ever since Elizabeth was a little girl, it had been her dream to be a writer. Getting her first article published in Sweet Valley High's student newspaper, the *Oracle,* had been a major event for her. But because she had started seeing Devon, she hadn't thought it was right to accept Todd's anniversary gift. Still, she cared about Todd. She had wanted to tell him that at the Dairi Burger—to ask him if they could still be friends.

"But Jessica had other plans," Elizabeth mumbled to herself as she paced. She and Todd had talked for a long while, a conversation full of feelings and memories that had reminded her of why she loved Todd in the first place. She'd begun to wonder if maybe Todd hadn't been right for her all along. As they had become more comfortable they had started to talk about the past week. Eventually she and Todd had put two and two together and realized Jessica had been behind the whole Courtney scheme.

It was at that moment that Jessica, Devon, and Courtney had stormed into the Dairi Burger. When Devon had seen Elizabeth with Todd, he'd lost it, and so had Todd. Devon, in a rage, had told Todd to leave Elizabeth alone. Todd, believing he was losing his one chance to get Elizabeth back, had dropped to his knees and proposed to her, offering her the silver ring to seal their engagement.

After that the situation had truly spiraled out of control. A shoving match had begun, and before Elizabeth had known what was happening, Devon and Todd had started fighting like a couple of Neanderthals. Elizabeth had begged someone to stop them—had even gotten bruised herself trying to break up the fight. It was humiliating and horrible. *How could both of them be such immature animals?* she had asked herself as she ran from the Dairi Burger. Todd, who was always so warm and considerate, Devon with his sensitive nature and brilliant mind?

Elizabeth flung out her hand angrily, knocking a slew of Todd's cards to the floor. *It's all Jessica's fault,* she told herself. *If she hadn't brought Devon and Courtney to the Dairi Burger, this would never have happened.* Jessica had done some pretty sleazy scheming in the past, but nothing this hateful.

Tears welled in Elizabeth's eyes, blurring the gifts and cards. She could never forgive Jessica for this—*never!* The tears came harder, and she flung herself onto the couch. Upstairs she could hear the shower running in the bathroom she and Jessica shared. The thought of Jessica going nonchalantly about her daily life after what she had done just made Elizabeth cry harder.

Burying her head in a throw pillow, Elizabeth wept her heart out. Suddenly through her sobs she heard the phone begin to ring. Her parents were out. She and Jessica were alone in the house, and Jessica would never hear the phone over the shower.

Elizabeth considered just letting the voice mail system take the call. *But what if it's important and the caller hangs up before the voice mail answers?* she thought. Swiping at her tears, she ran to the hallway and grabbed the receiver. "Hello?" she said in a shaky voice.

"Liz, finally!" It was Devon. "I've been trying to reach you all afternoon," he said. "I needed to tell you—"

Elizabeth cut him off. "There's nothing you can tell me I don't already know," she cried angrily. Then she slammed the receiver down, her tears breaking loose in a cascade of confusion and pain.

Sobbing, she ran upstairs toward her room. Jessica was just coming out of the bathroom. Her wavy blond hair was wrapped in a thick pink towel. She was wearing a fluffy white bathrobe and matching slippers, smiling contentedly as if everything was absolutely fine. Elizabeth shot her a furious look. "I hope you're happy!" she yelled. Then she ran into her bedroom, slamming the door behind her before she threw herself across the bed.

❖   ❖   ❖

Devon stared at the receiver, hearing the buzz of Elizabeth's disconnected line like the disappointing echo of his existence. His slate blue eyes flashed with pain as he dropped the receiver back in its cradle and paced the small but lovingly arranged room Nan had set up for him when he moved to Sweet Valley.

He smiled bitterly, recalling how he'd thought he'd finally found a home when he first came here. Nan Johnstone—his childhood nanny—had been his last refuge. For months Devon had been searching for a home, a place where he would be loved after his uncaring parents were killed in a car crash. His father's will had stipulated that Devon couldn't receive his full inheritance until he was twenty-one—four years from now—and then only if he found a guardian he could stay with for those four years.

Devon had considered forfeiting the inheritance. He had enough to live on without it, and money had so far given him more misery than happiness. But the truth was, Devon had desperately wanted a family, people who would care about him for who he was and not what he had. He'd thought a guardian might be just what he'd been looking for all his life.

He'd packed up and headed to his cousins' house in Ohio, where he had spent a fortune fixing up their house—"so he'd be comfortable" as his aunt Peggy kept assuring him—before he accepted the fact that they'd only been after his money.

After that he had headed out to find his uncle Pete in Las Vegas. He hadn't told his uncle about his inheritance, thinking that he would be able to figure out if Uncle Pete really cared for him or not.

As it turned out, Uncle Pete *wasn't* interested in his money—he wouldn't even let Devon help pay rent or expenses. Devon had thought he'd finally found someone who legitimately cared. But Uncle Pete was sneaky and had used Devon in other ways. Pete was a jewel thief and had tricked Devon into carrying stolen jewels to his partner.

After those two disastrous attempts at finding a guardian, Devon had all but given up. Then the letter came from Nan. At first he was suspicious. She hadn't contacted him in all the years since she'd left his father's employ. Why was she writing to him now? He couldn't help believing that she'd heard about his inheritance too and hoped to get her hands on some of it. But he'd come to Sweet Valley anyway, hoping against hope that he was wrong.

Then one day, when Nan was out, Devon had found a box of letters addressed to him, marked Return to Sender. It turned out Nan had been writing him letters for years and his parents had sent all her letters back, unopened. Nan had told him it was because his parents hadn't wanted him to be too dependent on her, but he knew she was being kind. The real reason was that they were jealous because Devon loved Nan more than he loved *them.* Devon shook his head in disgust. What had his parents expected? Nan was the only one who had ever cared about him.

Devon moved to the window, running an agitated hand through his thick dark hair. Outside, the North Star was rising above the palm tree in Nan's front yard. It wasn't so long ago, he recalled, that he'd watched that same star rise above his home in Westwood, Connecticut. Not so long ago that he would have said it had guided him to Sweet Valley—to Nan and Elizabeth.

Elizabeth. Just the thought of what he'd lost made him want to lash out in frustration and pain. When he'd found Elizabeth, he'd thought his luck had finally changed. His partner in chemistry lab, she was completely different from any girl he'd ever met—witty and smart and real. She wasn't interested in his money or the things he could give her. She wasn't interested in his Harley-Davidson motorcycle or his looks—just him.

But when he finally felt it was safe to open up, when he finally was beginning to allow himself to feel something, she had turned on him like all the others. How foolish of him to have left himself open like that. How dangerous.

Well, he told himself as he turned from the window, *it won't happen again.* From now on he would keep his distance, make sure his armor was good and strong. He might be alone forever, but he wouldn't be hurt again.

*   *   *

9

"Honestly," Jessica muttered as she examined the array of gifts and cards in the Wakefields' living room. "I don't know what all the fuss is about." Two of the cutest guys in school were begging Elizabeth to forgive them, sending her gifts, and she was acting like the world had come to an end.

Jessica tossed her sunny yellow hair over her shoulders and brushed a piece of lint off the pale blue and white sweater she'd pulled on to go with her jeans. Maybe she *had* gone a bit far, she conceded, but it wasn't all her fault. After all, she'd seen Devon first, in the parking lot of Sweet Valley High. As soon as their eyes had met she'd known she had to have him. And Elizabeth knew how strongly Jessica felt about Devon.

But Elizabeth had started digging her claws into Devon behind Jessica's back. She'd managed to steal Devon away even though she was still going out with Todd. Elizabeth had made a date to meet Devon at the Box Tree Café but backed out at the last minute, feeling guilty about Todd.

What infuriated Jessica more than anything was that Elizabeth had sent Jessica to meet Devon in her place but hadn't bothered to tell Jessica that Devon was expecting Elizabeth. It wasn't until Devon called Jessica Elizabeth that Jessica realized what had happened. Elizabeth had broken down and told Jessica the truth only after Jessica had made a fool of herself, pretending to be Elizabeth until she and Devon kissed and he figured it out.

It was Elizabeth's fault the date had gone bad, Jessica decided—Elizabeth's fault that Devon couldn't think of anyone but her. And now Elizabeth was blaming Jessica for everything that had happened to Todd and Devon and her. Like Jessica didn't have every right to get revenge on all three of them. It hadn't only been Elizabeth and Devon who'd treated her badly.

Jessica ripped the gold foil off Elizabeth's box of Belgian chocolates and popped one into her mouth, sinking down on the couch as the rich chocolate coated her tongue. It was as smooth as the plan she'd devised, she thought—definitely one of her better schemes.

"Too bad it completely backfired," Jessica muttered.

Todd had asked Jessica to help him get Elizabeth to the surprise publishing anniversary picnic he was planning for her. Even though Jessica knew Elizabeth was hot for Devon, for Todd's sake she had agreed. Elizabeth was supposed to meet Jessica at her locker after school, then Jessica was going to take Elizabeth to Todd's surprise picnic. But instead Jessica had found Devon and Elizabeth kissing in a playing field behind the school.

Furious, Jessica had driven to the beach where Todd had asked her to drop Elizabeth off. "Where's Elizabeth?" Todd had demanded when he realized the Wakefield twin coming toward him wasn't Elizabeth but Jessica.

11

Angrily, Jessica had told Todd about seeing Elizabeth and Devon together. "If we were to start going out together, we would completely shock Liz," she'd suggested, cozying up to Todd, wanting revenge. "She would get just what she deserves." What better way to get even than to make Elizabeth jealous of her own sister and boyfriend?

But Todd had refused to believe her and had left her sitting on the beach alone. *No one does that to Jessica Wakefield,* she reminded herself, popping another chocolate into her mouth.

That's when she'd hit on the Courtney Kane plan. *Todd's vulnerable,* she'd told Courtney. *You just happen to bump into him when he most needs to see a friendly face.* Jessica knew that once Elizabeth realized what she'd lost, she'd go running back to him—but with Courtney around, it would be too late. Then Jessica had learned that Elizabeth was meeting Todd at the Dairi Burger to tell him she still wanted to be friends. Jessica realized her whole plan would be ruined if Todd and Elizabeth put their heads together and figured out she was behind everything.

The only way to stop them was to have Courtney and Devon show up at the Dairi Burger at the same time as Elizabeth and Todd—let Courtney and Devon see what was happening behind their backs and put a stop to it. But it had been too late. By the time Devon and Courtney got there, Todd and Elizabeth had already figured out Jessica's scheme.

Of course, now everyone was furious with her. Elizabeth wasn't talking to her. Devon hated her. And Todd told Courtney he didn't want to see her anymore, so now Jessica had an enemy at a whole other school.

It's so unfair, Jessica thought, closing the box of chocolates. If Elizabeth was more like her, she'd see she had really gotten herself into this mess. Sure, the twins *looked* exactly alike, with their sun-streaked blond hair, blue-green eyes, and the same dimple in their left cheek. But that's where the similarities ended.

Jessica liked excitement and fun, and she did everything possible to make things that way. She was a cocaptain of the cheerleading squad, threw super parties, was totally active in the Pi Beta Alpha sorority, and loved looking as good as she felt, which meant shopping, shopping, shopping.

Elizabeth, on the other hand, lived a much more boring existence—reading books and writing for the *Oracle,* spending Saturday nights watching videos with her boyfriend. As for clothes, the more conservative the better was Elizabeth's motto. That was why Jessica could hardly believe Elizabeth had flirted with Devon behind Todd's back. Not that there was anything wrong with flirting—Jessica did it all the time. But Elizabeth had this weird thing about only going out with one guy at a time.

Still, Jessica couldn't help feeling bad that Elizabeth was ignoring her. Besides Lila Fowler,

Elizabeth was Jessica's best friend, and Jessica hated the cold shoulder she was getting from her sister. Not to mention the others.

Jessica tapped her forehead with a pale blue manicured nail. They all needed to lighten up, she decided. Now what could she do to hurry that along?

Her lips puckered in concentration and a few seconds later curled in a smile. *Of course, a party!* she concluded. She should have thought of it aeons ago. What everyone needed was a big barbecue party at Secca Lake. Music and dancing under the stars. It was *perfect!* Lila could help plan the menu and decorations, they'd get a live band—maybe the Droids—and all the cutest guys in school would come. Then they'd par-*tay* and everyone would stop taking things so seriously—Todd, Devon, *and* Elizabeth.

Jessica crossed her arms behind her head and sank deeper into the couch. *You're awesome, Jess,* she told herself, *simply amazing.* Now all she had to do was persuade Elizabeth to help, and in no time everything would be back to normal.

Chapter 2

Todd Wilkins stood in front of his locker at Sweet Valley High on Monday, pulling out his textbooks for his morning classes. He couldn't stop thinking about what a fool he'd made of himself Sunday afternoon. The Dairi Burger had been full of his classmates when he had fallen to his knees to propose to Elizabeth, and his fight with Devon Whitelaw had only added to his humiliation. He'd arrived at school early today so he wouldn't have to hang outside with his friends and deal with their ragging on him—or worse—feeling sorry for him.

He slammed his locker shut and started walking down the corridor toward the library. He'd hang out there until it was time for homeroom, he figured. No one would be at the library before school on a Monday morning.

A group of sophomores walked toward him as

he made his way past the chem labs. He recognized Zack Johnson, a linebacker on the Sweet Valley High football team, but most of them he only knew by sight.

The group seemed to be in a decent mood for a Monday morning. They were laughing, trading punches, talking about their weekend. Then one of them spotted Todd and nudged the guy beside him. They exchanged glances, and the conversation dwindled to nothing as they passed by—like Todd was a reject or something.

Todd felt the heat of embarrassment rise to his face. *Those guys must have heard about the Dairi Burger,* he thought. Great. Just great. School hadn't even started yet, and already he was getting the "loser" look. It was like living in a soap opera. First his girl dumps him for another guy, then—when there's this spark of a chance they'll be getting back together again—he loses it in a major way at a crowded restaurant and his girl dumps him for good.

He shook his head, staring at the floor. *At least no one saw me making a fool of myself pounding on Liz's door last night,* he told himself. The thought of it made him cringe.

Once the group of sophomores had disappeared around a corner, Todd started for the library again. The halls were empty except for a stray student here and there hanging around a locker or coming out of one of the rest rooms. Everyone else was chilling outside, eking out the last few minutes of freedom before a new school week started. That was something in his favor at least.

"Hey, Todd!" someone yelled just when Todd was about to duck into the safety of the library. He turned to his right and groaned. Caroline Pearce—the biggest gossip at Sweet Valley High—was coming toward him. *Just what I need,* he thought, running a hand through his short brown hair, *Caroline prying even deeper into what I'm trying to forget.*

"Todd!" Caroline called out, breathless. "I've been looking all *over* for you! I heard what happened at the Dairi Burger, and I figured, well, you *must* just be *devastated.*" Caroline's eyes were gleaming like a predator's ready for the kill.

"How's it goin'?" Todd muttered, averting his coffee brown eyes to avoid locking gazes with Caroline. Before Caroline could answer, he said, "Uh, look, I've got an appointment with my guidance counselor. I gotta go."

"But To-oodd . . . ," Caroline whined. Todd ignored her, spun around, and headed the other way.

He hadn't gone ten feet when suddenly Elizabeth turned the corner, flanked by Maria Slater and Enid Rollins. Elizabeth looked beautiful. Her hair was pulled back to show off her delicate features. She was wearing an ocean blue blouse that he knew would pick up the color of her eyes if she were closer.

17

Todd's heart raced at the sight of her. He wanted so badly to be with her, to hold her, to feel his lips on hers again. But after the Dairi Burger and the incident at her house last night, he wouldn't blame her for thinking he was a major buffoon.

He swung around the other way. Caroline Pearce was rushing toward him, ready to pounce. He glanced back toward Elizabeth and her friends. Elizabeth would spot him at any moment, and he just couldn't stand to face her right now.

Frantic, Todd looked for a way out. There was an exit door a few feet to his left. It was his only option.

In one second flat he was out the door and on the cafeteria delivery ramp. Hanging out on the ramp were Keith Wagner, Aaron Dallas, Bruce Patman, and Winston Egbert—just about everyone he was trying to avoid. *Well,* he thought, realizing he was trapped, *it's too late now.*

"Hey, Todd, how are you?" Winston asked solemnly. Winston was the class clown. Usually he'd be making some weird face or cracking a joke. Now he was as serious as the rest of them.

"Great," Todd lied. "Everything's great."

Bruce and Aaron exchanged the same look he'd seen on the sophomores' faces a few minutes earlier. Todd wondered how he was going to make it through this day with everyone tiptoeing around him and talking behind his back. A surge of anger shot through him. "Look," he said, "if any of you has something to say, then say it, all right?"

The guys gave each other meaningful looks, but no one said a word.

Keith—who was a peace-and-love type—seemed turned off by the way the guys were treating Todd. "Oh, you guys are real cool," he said in an annoyed voice. "Can't you see the man's in pain? Like none of you has ever done something you wished you hadn't." He shook his head.

Bruce rolled his eyes, but Aaron and Winston seemed kind of embarrassed.

Keith stepped forward and clapped Todd on the shoulder, smiling that ultraserene smile of his. *He could be standing under a tidal wave,* Todd thought, *and he'd still be smiling, flashing everyone the peace sign.*

"Listen, man," Keith said, shaking his dark brown hair out of his eyes. "I know you're hurting, but you gotta try to get over it." He nodded at this, like he was agreeing with himself. "Love's a funny thing, man," he continued. "You did what you had to do when you had to do it. Enough said."

Todd shook his head. "I've made a mess of everything," he said despondently. "Liz hates me. I'm the number-one reject in school. . . ." He shot a look at the other guys. "Even my friends don't know what to say to me." His hands curled into fists. "I just wish Devon Whitelaw had never set foot in Sweet Valley," he spat.

"Hey, bro," Keith said, dropping his hands palms

19

down in a calming gesture. "That kind of attitude will just eat away at your spirit. Things happen in life, man. You've got to face the fact that Elizabeth did what she wanted to do, and there's nothing you could have done to change it. What you need to do now is loosen up. Release all that aggression and hostility. You gotta let go of the past, man."

Winston, who'd been leaning against the ramp rail, stood up straight and began rubbing his chin in an authoritative manner. "The young man's got a point," he said in a deep bass voice, the clownish glint back in his eyes.

Todd ignored him. "Let go of the past?" he repeated. "Does that mean I should let go of Elizabeth too?" He shook his head, dwelling momentarily on what Keith had said about Elizabeth doing what she wanted to do. Maybe she had, Todd decided, but she wouldn't have done it if Devon Whitelaw hadn't been around. "The fact is," Todd told Keith, "I don't want to let go of Liz. I want her back."

"Right on," Aaron said, giving him a thumbs-up.

"All I'm saying," Keith explained, shooting Aaron a look, "is that you've got to live for today. Let your spirit *roam*."

Todd's eyes narrowed with suspicion. He liked Keith, but there was no denying the guy was a hippie type with weird New Age ideas. "What exactly do you mean, 'let my spirit roam'? You want me to beat on drums? Howl at the moon?"

20

Keith grinned. "Not a bad idea, bro," he said. "But I'm talking about something a little more down-to-earth. Mountain biking."

"Mountain biking?" Bruce repeated, looking at Keith incredulously.

"Yeah, man. A bunch of us guys get together and go riding every afternoon before sunset," Keith replied.

Todd did a double take. Keith and *sports?* He'd have thought the most athletic thing Keith would do was yoga. "I didn't know you were into sports," he said.

"Sure," Keith told him. "Mountain biking's extreme. Natural high, man. Good for what ails you." He leaned in closer to Todd. "And no ladies. So no ladies to worry about."

"Sounds decent," Aaron said.

"Except for the no-ladies part," Bruce emphasized.

Winston rolled his eyes. "That's the whole point, dude!" he exclaimed with a goofy surfer's accent. The guys laughed.

"So you want to come along?" Keith asked Todd.

Todd shrugged. "I don't know, Keith," he said. "How's biking in the woods with a pack of guys going to win Elizabeth back for me?"

"Hey, you never know until you try," Keith philosophized. "Besides, what have you got to lose? You can't lose what you don't have—and I hate to say it, man, but you definitely don't have Elizabeth anymore."

Just then the late bell rang. "I'll think about it," Todd told Keith as the group of them headed to homeroom. But hard as he tried, all he could really think about was Elizabeth.

Devon grabbed his chemistry book from his locker and checked around the corridor. The hall was packed with students, some hurrying to their first-period classes, some leaning against the lockers, a couple in front of him making out—but no Elizabeth. He slammed his locker door shut, scowling at the happy couple. Where was she? Their chemistry class started in a few minutes. Elizabeth's locker was right down the hall from his, but he hadn't seen her yet.

An icy finger jabbed at his spine. Was Elizabeth avoiding him? Was that what was happening? His grip tightened on his chemistry book. Well, she couldn't avoid him forever. They were in chem lab together. When he saw her, he'd explain. She'd have to listen to him. She'd have to understand. . . .

Determined to make things right, Devon strode purposefully down the corridor to chem lab. But when he walked through the door, Elizabeth wasn't there. Instead a nerdy-looking guy with chopped brown hair and black glasses was sitting in Elizabeth's seat. Devon marched up to him. "I think you've got the wrong seat," he said, trying to control his annoyance.

The nerdy guy shook his head. "Nope," he told Devon. "I was transferred from another chem lab and they assigned me to this seat. The girl who used to sit here requested another lab," he explained.

Devon felt his blood boil. How could Elizabeth do this to him? They had so much in common, a real chemistry. Now she wouldn't even sit in the same room with him.

Angry and hurt, he slammed his book down on the table and headed for the door. "Where are you going?" his new lab partner asked. "We're supposed to experiment with flash explosions today."

Devon smiled bitterly. "You'll have to handle it alone," he said. "I'm obviously not very good at chemistry." He stormed out of the room. *If Liz can forget our feelings for each other so easily,* he thought, *then so can I*. But the ache in his heart hurt worse than ever.

Heading out to the parking lot, Devon hopped on his motorcycle and roared away from the high school. He had to get out of there. Far away. But where was there left to go?

He finally headed to the lookout point where he'd first gone on arriving in Sweet Valley—a place where, for a moment, he'd actually felt a bit of hope, a glimmer of happiness.

Parking his bike on the ridge, he walked to the edge of the cliff. Below him lay Sweet Valley, and beyond, the sparkling Pacific. He recalled how he'd first felt when he'd seen the valley and ocean, how he'd allowed himself to believe that—maybe this time—things would work out for him.

Now, as he gazed at the town below, he didn't see the tree-lined streets and pretty, well-kept houses so much as the betrayal that lay behind their doors. How could he stay here, see Elizabeth every day and not be able to be with her? His solution to hurt had always been to run. Run from his controlling parents. Run from his greedy cousins. Run from his conniving uncle. Make a new start.

But he'd journeyed all the way across the country to get here. And Nan was the first person in his life who had felt like a real family to him. Where could he possibly go next?

He stared across the valley to the blue-green ocean. His whole life seemed to have been one big disappointment, one sorry mistake. As he watched the rolling waves crash to shore he wondered if maybe it wouldn't be better for everyone if he just kept going—just rode straight into the crashing surf and disappeared.

"It's going to be amazing," Jessica cooed. "I'm thinking of a tropical theme—lanterns, barbecued food, and music under the stars . . . totally romantic," Jessica gushed, glancing at Aaron Dallas, who was sitting across the cafeteria table from her, eating a roast beef sub. Aaron was definitely cute, with a sexy grin and an athletic soccer player's

24

body. Jessica had dated him several times in the past. She smiled coyly at him, smoothing down the front of her pink silk T-shirt, and Aaron returned the smile.

"Just what is this party for again?" Amy asked, fiddling with a few strands of her ash-blond shoulder-length hair.

"Well," Jessica explained, leaning across the table. "Liz and Todd are really in the dumps over this Dairi Burger fiasco, and it's leaving *me* in the dumps. I figured a huge party would cheer us all up!"

"Sounds like an awful lot of work," Maria Santelli interjected.

Jessica nodded, glancing approvingly at the fitted emerald green sweater Maria was wearing. It worked well with her dark features. Jessica took a delicate bite of her chef's salad. "Oh, it *is* a lot of work," she agreed. She glanced at Lila. "Of course, I'm sure I'll have help. Some of my best friends are *incredible* at arranging social events and wheedling awesome recipes for honey Dijon ribs from their chefs."

Lila brushed a crumb from her charcoal gray Louis Féraud suit jacket and tossed back her light brown wavy hair. "You're about as subtle as a hurricane, Jess," she said drolly. "Just when do you propose to throw this hoedown anyway?"

Jessica frowned. "Barbecue," she corrected Lila. "And I'm planning to do it a week from

Saturday to give us plenty of time to make arrangements."

Lila groaned. "Less than two weeks for a party the size of Sweet Valley? That's plenty of time, all right."

"Well, if you don't want to help. . . ." Jessica pouted, looking hurt.

Lila sighed. "Of course I'll help," she replied.

"Great," Jessica said, perking right up again. "One of the first things I'll need you to do is help me get Liz involved," Jessica told her. "This slump she's in is driving me *crazy*."

"Short drive," Bruce Patman quipped. Amy giggled.

"Oh, that's so *clever*, Bruce," Jessica said sarcastically. Bruce came from one of the richest families in Sweet Valley, but aside from his good looks and money, he was a real drag as far as Jessica was concerned. "But I'm serious," she added. "This slump of Liz's is really getting to me."

"Elizabeth wouldn't be in a slump if it wasn't for your interference," Lila reminded Jessica.

Jessica waved the comment away. "That's ridiculous," she said. "And besides, if I remember correctly, you were in on the Courtney-Todd operation too. On top of which," she added, "*I* saw Devon first. Liz shouldn't have gotten in the way."

Bruce got up from the table. "I'm gettin' while the gettin's good," he said.

Aaron laughed. "Coward," he jibed.

Jessica made a face. "Let's put it this way," she

said. "Maybe I'm not *entirely* innocent, but Liz had as much to do with this mess as I did. Of course, I'm willing to let bygones be bygones if Liz is."

"Big of you," Maria said.

Jessica rolled her eyes. "Give me a break," she retorted. "I know my sister as well as I know my way around the mall. She'll snap out of it. This party's just the thing Liz needs."

Amy took a sip of milk. "I think it sounds pretty cool," she said. "It'll give me a good excuse to buy that cute sarong I saw at the Unique Boutique, right, Barry?"

Barry Rork, Amy's boyfriend, shook his head. "As long as you don't try to get me into a Hawaiian shirt," he said. The guys laughed.

"Winston will wear a Hawaiian shirt if I ask him to, won't you, Winston?" Maria asked jokingly.

Winston got up and started to do a hula. "Anything you say, lani-luni," he said. Maria laughed.

"Count me in," Aaron told Jessica.

Jessica smiled. The ball was really rolling. Now all she needed was a date. *Who'll be the lucky guy to take me to the party?* she wondered, glancing around the table.

Her eyes met Aaron's again. He winked. *Maybe . . . ,* she thought. *He's such a good dancer.* She tapped her chin with the tip of a fingernail. *Who else?* she wondered, swinging her leg back and forth. Her eyes roamed the table. There were cute guys *every*where, she realized.

Devon isn't the only fish in the sea, she told herself.

Now, if only she could get Elizabeth to help with the plans. . . .

"So what happened after Devon and Todd started fighting?" Enid asked Elizabeth as they left the SVH parking lot Monday afternoon on their way to the Great Mountain National Reserve. Enid, Elizabeth's best friend, had wanted to go to the Dairi Burger, but Elizabeth was afraid Todd or Devon would be there, and she didn't want to see either of them. "Let's take a ride somewhere," Elizabeth had suggested, and Enid had come up with the Great Mountain Reserve.

As they drove toward the mountains Elizabeth recapped the whole sordid Dairi Burger story. "It was horrible," she concluded. "I thought I knew Todd and Devon, but they really showed their true colors that night. And Jess!" Elizabeth shook her head in disgust. "Jessica's pulled some sorry stunts before, but *this*—I don't think I'll ever forgive her for this one."

They arrived at the Great Mountain parking lot, and Enid stopped the car. There was a picnic area a hundred feet or so away. Elizabeth and Enid followed a narrow path to a rust-colored picnic table and sat down. A couple of robins were flitting between pine trees, chirping and chasing each other. "It's a mating ritual," Enid explained. "I saw it on

Nature's Wonders. Birds always have these elaborate courting practices."

"Please," Elizabeth said, waving away the conversation. "No talk about courting."

Enid pushed her shoulder-length, curly reddish brown hair behind her ears and glanced sideways at Elizabeth. "Sorry, Liz," she said.

They watched the birds some more, and Elizabeth began to relax. "Ah, this is more like it," she gushed, stretching her legs in front of her. "A place where I can think. You know," she said, "it really feels good being out here in the wild. My head feels so much clearer."

Enid nodded. "It's the fresh air," she commented. "Cleans out the brain cells."

"I guess," Elizabeth agreed, "but it's more than that. It's so peaceful—no noise, no problems . . . no guys." She sighed. "It's like I need to get away from everything," she continued. "I need to figure out what I'm doing and where I'm going, but it's impossible to do that when I can't get a moment alone to think." She fingered a knothole on the picnic table's surface. "I feel like I need to start fresh," she added introspectively. "To do something I've never done before—something on my own. Something I wouldn't do with Todd or Devon."

"Like what?" Enid asked.

Elizabeth shrugged. "I don't know," she said with a sigh of frustration. "It's just a feeling."

They watched a couple of gray squirrels

playing near the picnic bench for a moment.

"You know," Enid said casually, breaking the silence as she picked up an acorn to feed the squirrels. "My cousin went on a Project Adventure trip here to try to figure out what he wanted to do with his life."

"Project Adventure?" Elizabeth said. "What's that?"

"It's a bonding-with-nature thing," Enid explained. "A group goes out into the woods and learns to survive by using the natural elements around them. They stay together for a few days, then go solo for a night in the wilderness. It's supposed to test your limits," she continued. "To teach you to draw on your inner strength."

Enid gently tossed her acorn toward the squirrels. "Of course," she added, "it's not something *I'd* want to do. My cousin actually had to catch a rabbit and *eat* it," she concluded, her face twisted with disgust.

Elizabeth hardly noticed. "Project Adventure, huh?" she said, intrigued. "How do you get to go on one of those trips?"

"I guess you just have to sign up," Enid said. "The Project Adventure phone number is in the book." She shuddered. "Can you imagine killing and eating a *rabbit*? It's so *weird*. But then, my cousin's kind of weird too," she added, tossing another acorn to the squirrels.

"I don't think it's so weird," Elizabeth said.

"How do you know what your limits are unless you push them? And what better way to push them than to survive a night alone in the wilderness?" Her forehead wrinkled in thought. "I think I'd like to find out more about this organization."

"You mean Project Adventure? Why? Are you planning to write about it for the *Oracle*?" Enid asked.

Elizabeth shrugged. "Maybe. Or maybe I was thinking it wouldn't be such a bad thing to experience."

"*Experience?*" Enid said, looking at her as if she were crazy. The squirrels, startled by Enid's outburst, scampered away. "Look, Liz," Enid told her, "I just mentioned it in passing. I didn't mean for you to take the suggestion seriously!" She shook her head in disbelief. "This whole guy thing must have really gotten to you." Her eyes searched Elizabeth's face. "You're all right, aren't you?" Enid asked with concern. "I mean, you're not thinking of doing anything stupid."

Elizabeth smiled. "Don't be so narrow-minded, Enid. I'm just trying to find where my inner strength lies," she said. "And this Project Adventure trip just might be the perfect way to do it." She glanced at Enid's shocked face and couldn't help laughing. "Hear me roar!" she joked, nudging Enid in the ribs.

Chapter 3

"Tropical, definitely tropical. We're looking for lots of bright colors—parrots, exotic flowers, stuff like that," Jessica informed Lila as they rode the escalator to the second floor of the Valley Mall.

It was Tuesday afternoon. Jessica and Lila had left for the mall right after school to start searching for decorations for the Secca Lake party. They were headed for the Paper Tiger, a party shop that had the best variety of party items in Sweet Valley.

"And we have to think of a way to get Elizabeth involved in the party plans," Jessica added as they stepped off the escalator. "She's still pretty upset. It'll be the best thing for her."

Lila raised an eyebrow. "What do *I* have to do with it?" she demanded. "And anyway, from what I've heard, I doubt anything short of you dropping your knees and begging Liz's forgiveness will work."

"Forget it," Jessica huffed. "I had every right to do what I did. After all, Liz stole Devon from *me*."

Lila rolled her eyes. "Whatever," she said.

They reached the Paper Tiger, and Lila's attention was drawn to some stirrers sitting on a shelf by the door. "Ooo, *these* are cute!" she said, picking up a package of drinking straws shaped like tropical fruits.

"We're having cans of soda, not mixed drinks, Li," Jessica said impatiently.

Lila tapped her chin with a French-manicured nail. "Maybe I could have the chef whip up some kind of tropical freeze," she suggested.

Jessica looked dubious. "He'd have to make *gallons*," she said. "And how are we going to keep it frozen? No refrigerators at the lake."

Lila sighed. "I suppose you're right," she said, moving on to the paper plate section. "I keep forgetting this party's on a budget." She picked up a package of red, blue, and yellow plates covered with tropical birds and flora. "How about these?"

Jessica dropped the napkins she was looking at. "Perfect!" she exclaimed. "Are there matching table accessories?"

Lila fanned through the rows of napkins and tablecloths. "Here they are!" she announced, pulling out a package of complementary tableware.

"Super," Jessica said, and her forehead wrinkled with concentration. "Six packages of napkins and plates are enough, you think?"

"That's a hundred and twenty plates and two hundred and forty napkins," Lila calculated. "I think it'll do."

"Cool," Jessica said, loading the supplies into a red plastic carrier she'd picked up at the door.

"How about invitations?" Lila asked. "You don't want just anybody showing up."

Jessica nodded. "Good point," she agreed.

They walked over to the card section and began to look through the invitations. There were clown-and-pony cards for little kids' birthday parties, frilly wedding invitations, and pastel-colored baby shower cards, but nothing for a tropical party at the lake.

"I can talk to the designer who prints my parents' party invitations," Lila told Jessica. "It's short notice, but for the right price he'll do them for us."

Jessica raised an eyebrow. "How much is the 'right price'?" she asked.

Lila shrugged. "Five or six hundred dollars, depending on how many you want to send out."

"Five or six *hundred!*" Jessica exclaimed. "That's way out of my range. There won't be enough left for the food and the band. And I've already dipped way deep into my clothing allowance as it is."

"OK, bad idea," Lila conceded, thumbing through the cards. "How about these?" she suggested, holding up a white invitation with gold lettering—*The pleasure of your company is requested at . . .*

35

Jessica wrinkled her nose. "Too stuffy," she said.

Lila pulled out a card with brightly colored balloons spelling out *It's a party!* "What do you think of this one?" Lila asked.

Jessica shook her head. "Ultrahokey," she concluded.

They sorted through the rest of the cards without any luck.

"So what do you propose we do?" Lila asked impatiently. "I refuse to go to every party store in Sweet Valley, looking for invitations."

Jessica frowned. "There's got to be *something . . . ,*" she said. Suddenly she grabbed Lila's arm. "Hey, wait a minute!" she exclaimed excitedly. "Why don't we make our *own* invitations?"

Lila shot her a sardonic look. "Get real," she said. "How are we going to do that?"

Jessica smiled slyly. "Easy. We ask Olivia Davidson to paint a tropical scene for us. You know what a good painter she is." Olivia was the arts editor for the *Oracle,* and both Jessica and Lila had seen a few of her paintings in the *Oracle* office.

Lila nodded. "OK, so Olivia gives us an illustration. What do we write on it? You don't seem to like anything here," she pointed out, flinging a hand toward the stack of cards they'd gone through.

Jessica gave her a smug look. "That's the best part," she said. "We get Liz to write something clever to go with Olivia's picture."

36

Lila took a deep breath. "I don't know," she said skeptically. "It seems like a long shot, if you ask me."

"No way," Jessica retorted. "Liz is practically obsessed when it comes to writing. She can barely walk by a pad of paper without scribbling something down. She won't be able to refuse."

Jessica threw some plastic dinnerware into the carrier as she led Lila to the cash register. "Once Olivia and Liz have done their thing," she continued, "we can take the finished product to the Copy Mart and have custom-designed invitations for a *smidgen* of the price your designer would charge us."

Lila piled the napkins onto the checkout counter. "I have to admit, it does sound like a pretty good idea," she conceded.

"It's a *great* idea," Jessica corrected her. She placed the empty carrier with some others beside the counter. "Sometimes I even amaze myself," she added with a smile.

Alone on the basketball court, Todd eyed the hoop from the foul line and shot. The ball flew through the air and bounced off the backboard, missing the hoop by a good six inches. He tried again. This time he barely hit the net. Todd shook his head, then ran toward the basket for a slam dunk. The ball bounced off the rim and back onto the court. *Great*, Todd thought. *The way I'm playing, I couldn't even compete against a grade-school player.*

He left the court and plopped down on the bleachers, his head in his hands. No matter what he did, he couldn't stop thinking about Elizabeth. It was so depressing. He'd tried everything to distract himself—marathon TV, magazines, loud music. He'd even tried to lose himself in research for the history term paper due in a month—to no avail. He needed way more distraction to dull his pain, but what?

With a sigh Todd pushed himself up and left the court, halfheartedly dribbling the basketball as he headed for his car. When he reached his BMW, he climbed in and leaned his head against the headrest. *There's got to be something I can do to get Liz back,* he thought. But he'd sent gifts, begged for forgiveness—what else was there *to* do?

He shook his head. This was bad news for sure. He and Elizabeth had had their problems before— like her fling with that Joey Mason guy from Camp Echo Mountain. Now that had been bad. He'd actually caught them kissing. And then there was his flirtation with Peggy Abbot. They'd gone out on a date but decided they were better as friends than as a couple.

But those things had always blown over. His and Elizabeth's love had always been strong enough to see them through the rough times. But this time—well, he'd never seen Elizabeth like this. She'd never refused to even listen to him before, to even *look* at him. What if he could never get her back?

He pulled out of the school parking lot and headed toward the ocean. He needed someplace quiet to think. If he could just forget about Elizabeth for a while, get things in perspective . . .

As he rounded a curve on the road to the beach Todd noticed a bunch of guys on racing bikes taking a water break along the side of the road. Their T-shirts were plastered to their backs with sweat. They were all smiling, patting each other on their backs, giving each other high fives.

Todd felt a twinge of envy. It reminded him of the way he felt about his basketball games when he was pushing his limit, the high he got from the exertion and team spirit, the mellow feeling coming down from the game. Or the way he *used* to feel. Even *that* hadn't been doing it for him since his breakup with Elizabeth.

As he passed the group he recalled Keith's invitation to go mountain biking. He really hadn't planned on taking Keith up on it, but maybe he should give mountain biking a try. It was about the only thing left he *hadn't* tried. And anything had to be better than sitting home miserable, thinking about Elizabeth. He glanced in his rearview mirror at the bikers. *Anything.*

On Tuesday evening Jessica and her parents waited at the dining-room table for Elizabeth. Jessica was starving. She hadn't eaten a bite since lunch. "Maybe Elizabeth's not hungry," she suggested impatiently to her parents.

Mrs. Wakefield glanced at Mr. Wakefield. "Elizabeth's hardly eaten a thing since this boyfriend dilemma began," she said worriedly.

Jessica rolled her eyes. Her mom could pass for the twins' sister with her blond hair, blue eyes, and slender build. And she was great at interior decorating. Her taste and business sense were really sharp, which explained why her interior design business was such a success. But sometimes she was as clueless as Principal Chrome Dome when it came to handling a teenager. Elizabeth wasn't a piece of glass. She wasn't going to break.

"Give her a few more minutes," her dad said, reaching for a piece of bread.

A moment later Elizabeth came bounding into the dining room. Her complexion was glowing, and there was a slight smile on her face. *She's obviously in a better mood than she's been in since the Dairi Burger disaster,* Jessica thought. *Maybe I won't have to sell the Secca Lake party so hard after all.*

Elizabeth sat down. "Sorry to keep you waiting," she told her parents. "I was talking to Enid and lost track of time."

Mrs. Wakefield smiled. "That's all right, sweetie." She picked up a platter of pot roast and handed it to her husband. "Ned?" she said.

Mr. Wakefield took a couple of slices of pot roast and passed the platter to Elizabeth, who forked two huge slices of meat onto her plate.

Cool, Jessica thought. *Liz's appetite is back.* She smiled smugly to herself. Elizabeth had probably realized that Jessica had been right all along and come to grips with it. Jessica picked up a bowl of vegetables. "Carrots?" she asked, offering the bowl to Elizabeth.

Elizabeth shook her head coolly and turned away.

"Fine, more for me," Jessica snapped, spooning a pile of carrots onto her plate.

"So how was school today?" her mom asked, changing the subject.

Jessica shrugged. "Boring as usual," she said, stuffing some carrots into her mouth.

Her mother frowned. "There's more to life than boys and parties, Jessica," she said sternly.

"Really?" Jessica said with an impish grin. "I hadn't noticed."

Her mother sighed, shaking her head with a mixture of affection and exasperation. "And how was your day, Liz?" she asked.

Elizabeth glanced disdainfully at Jessica. "Surprisingly *I* actually *learned* something today," she said sarcastically. "Do you know there's still a Stone Age tribe of people living in South America, making tools and living off the land like our ancestors did thousands of years ago? Isn't that *something?*"

"It is hard to believe," her father said. "People depending only on their wits and a few meager tools to survive in the wild."

Elizabeth laid down her fork. "I think they can really teach us something," she said. "I mean, we've all kind of lost touch with our survival instincts, don't you think? We get food at the supermarket, buy our clothes at department stores . . ."

"Preferably boutiques," Jessica interjected. "And anyone who's been through a clearance sale at Kiki's has to have pretty good survival instincts to make it out alive."

Mr. and Mrs. Wakefield laughed, but Elizabeth ignored her.

"What I'm trying to say," Elizabeth told her parents, "is that I think it's important for us to get back in touch with our natural selves. To learn how to rely on our inner resources."

"Oh, please," Jessica muttered, pushing a piece of potato around her plate.

But her father looked tickled. "That's a very mature outlook, Elizabeth," he said. "Nature is a great teacher."

"Exactly!" Elizabeth agreed. "Which is why I became interested in this Project Adventure program."

"Project Adventure?" her mom repeated, head cocked to one side. "What's that?"

Mr. Wakefield scratched his chin. "I believe there was a write-up on that in the *Sweet Valley News* a while ago," he answered thoughtfully. "Some sort of wilderness survival thing, isn't it?"

Elizabeth nodded. "It's an amazing program," she told her parents. "Enid mentioned that her cousin went on a Project Adventure outing, and it got me thinking. When I got home, I looked up their number in the phone book and spoke to one of the Project Adventure guides. He told me that the typical Project Adventure outing lasts for a week. A group of people go to the Great Mountain National Reserve and learn how to live in the wild—identify plants and wildlife, track animals, and build fires without so much as a match! It ends with an overnight solo, each person alone in the woods with only a compass, a pocketknife, and a sleeping bag. He said it really tests a person's limits."

"It sounds disgusting," Jessica said, wrinkling her nose.

Elizabeth didn't acknowledge the comment. "In any case," she said to her parents, "I've decided I want to do it."

Jessica stared at Elizabeth, mouth agape. Was Elizabeth *crazy?* A week without telephones, TV, or lights? Without running water, a bed, or a hot meal?

Mr. and Mrs. Wakefield exchanged glances. "Isn't it a bit dangerous?" Mrs. Wakefield asked, her forehead wrinkling doubtfully.

Elizabeth shook her head. "Not really," she told her mother. "They give you a beeper in case of an emergency."

Alice Wakefield looked doubtful. "A beeper isn't going to protect you against a bear attack," she pointed out.

43

"They teach you how to avoid wild animals," Elizabeth argued. "I asked the guide. He said no one's ever gotten more than a few mosquito bites and some scratches."

"I don't know . . . ," her mother said, glancing toward Mr. Wakefield.

"Please," Elizabeth begged. "There's one spot left, and I really want to do this."

Her parents looked at each other for a moment, then her mother said hesitantly, "Well, you've always made wise decisions in the past. And it sounds like this could be a good thing. . . ."

Elizabeth glanced anxiously at her father.

"If it's all right with your mother, it's all right with me," he told her. "According to the article in the newspaper, people come back much more clearheaded and psychologically stronger. Able to face adversity head-on." His forehead wrinkled thoughtfully. "As long as you're certain you'll be safe," he added.

"I'm certain," Elizabeth assured him excitedly. Then a tentative look crossed her face, and she added hesitantly, "There is one problem—I'll have to take a week off school."

Mrs. Wakefield looked at her a moment, then leaned over and whispered something in Mr. Wakefield's ear. He nodded.

Mrs. Wakefield smiled at Elizabeth. "If this Project Adventure is everything you say it is, your father and I think the knowledge you'll gain from

44

the experience will be well worth the time you miss," she reported.

"*What!*" Jessica exclaimed, staring at her parents incredulously. "You're letting her take a whole week off *school?*"

"It'll be an educational experience," her mom explained.

"That's right. Experience is the best teacher," Mr. Wakefield said.

Jessica's mouth dropped open in amazement. Had they *all* gone nuts? Elizabeth begging to be allowed out in the wilderness with a bunch of Tarzan and Jane wanna-bes? And their parents letting her take a week off school to *do* it? Jessica pushed her plate away indignantly. She couldn't imagine them cutting *her* that kind of slack for something *she* wanted to do. Of course, a week with bugs and bees was about the farthest thing from her wish list.

"Well," Mrs. Wakefield said, pushing away from the table. "It looks like we're finished here. Anybody want coffee?"

"I'd love some," Mr. Wakefield answered, getting up to help her clear the dishes.

Jessica and Elizabeth both declined and got up from the table. "Need some help?" Elizabeth asked her parents.

Her mother shook her head. "You girls can clean up tomorrow."

Once their parents had gone, Jessica followed

45

Elizabeth out of the dining room, catching up with her in the hallway. "Are you ever going to talk to me again?" she asked Elizabeth's back.

Elizabeth stopped in her tracks, her shoulders tensing, but said nothing.

"Look," Jessica said. "A week in the woods with a bunch of bugs will be pure *torture*. Mad as I am about Devon and you, I didn't mean to punish you *that* much."

Elizabeth whipped around, her eyes flashing with rage. "Then just how much *did* you mean to punish me?" she shot back, answering Jessica for the first time in days.

Jessica crossed her arms defensively. "You know, Liz," she said angrily, "you *did* steal Devon from me in the sleaziest way. I have a right to be furious."

Elizabeth snorted in disgust. "You can *have* Devon after the way he acted at the Dairi Burger," she declared.

Jessica scowled. "He's still hopelessly in love with *you*, walking the school halls all moody and wounded," she responded bitterly.

For an instant the look on Elizabeth's face changed from anger to pain. Jessica could see she'd gotten to her twin.

But then Elizabeth shook her head, as if to banish all feelings of Devon. "You don't seem to be hurting for male companionship anyway," she retorted. "Enid told me she saw you surrounded by guys at lunch yesterday."

Jessica was about to throw a sarcastic comeback but changed her mind. Why push this thing any further? Besides, Elizabeth's mentioning the guys was a perfect opportunity to introduce her to the Secca Lake party plan.

"This is silly, Liz," Jessica said in a much calmer tone. "We shouldn't be fighting. If you want to know the truth, the reason I was with all those guys yesterday is that I was telling them about this *fabulous* barbecue I'm planning for the Saturday after this at Secca Lake. Naturally I'd love for you to help me. . . ."

"You want *me* to help *you* plan a *party?*" Elizabeth blurted, gaping at Jessica in disbelief.

"Sure, why not?" Jessica said. "It'll be fun!"

Elizabeth's expression went from heated anger to icy disdain. She stared at Jessica a moment, her blue-green eyes cold as icebergs. "You don't get it, do you?" she said frostily. "Just the thought of hanging around with a bunch of couples at a lakeside barbecue makes me ill."

Elizabeth turned to go upstairs, but Jessica blocked her way, making one last-ditch attempt to get Elizabeth involved. "OK, so maybe you're not in the most sociable mood," she conceded. "But I can't plan this party without you, Liz," she cajoled. "I need you to help with the preparations. You always remember things everyone else forgets, like napkins or spare light bulbs for the lanterns," she added, hoping flattery would change Elizabeth's mind.

"Forget it," Elizabeth said, pushing past her.

"Wait!" Jessica yelled as Elizabeth started up the stairs.

Elizabeth stopped and turned to face her twin. "What?" she asked coldly, folding her arms over her chest.

Jessica studied her sister's rigid expression. *It's time to pull out the big guns,* she decided. "Liz, the truth is, I need someone to write the invitations," she blurted. "No one can write like you," she said, piling the flattery on thick in the hope of changing Elizabeth's mind. "If you don't want to help with anything else, just help me with that," she concluded, knowing Elizabeth couldn't refuse.

But she was wrong. Elizabeth didn't even blink. "I don't want to have anything to do with your party, Jessica," she said. "Find someone else to manipulate." With that, Elizabeth climbed the stairs to her room, leaving Jessica staring after her.

The sun was just beginning to set when Devon made his way to Jackson's Bluff, a remote spot near the ocean where he could be alone. The bottom of his jeans were wet from the surf, and his muscular arms were bared to the sun's dwindling rays as he trudged despondently across the wet sand.

He watched the splashes of reflected sun drifting on the rolling blue water and recalled how yesterday he had considered ending it all. He'd actually gone so far as to ride his Harley-Davidson down to the ocean. But once he was there, he had changed his mind. As lousy as he felt, giving up now would only mean all those people who had caused him pain in the past would win.

If anything happened to him, his greedy cousins and his uncle Pete would be sure to get a good chunk of his money after the custodians appointed by his father had taken their share. Even if Elizabeth cared enough to cry over his demise, she'd cry in Todd's arms. And his death would devastate Nan.

No, the thing to do was hit the road again, he told himself, settling wearily on some damp rocks. See if there was someplace he could find where he fit in, where he wouldn't be disappointed again. But where? He'd traveled across the country, and it had been the same everywhere. *Maybe I should just become a hermit,* he thought bitterly. *Build a log cabin in the wilds of Montana or Canada—someplace without people and the pain they cause.*

He ran his hands through his hair, watching the sun dip lower behind the water. As the clouds turned from pale pink to deep purple a lone seagull flew across the horizon. Devon followed it with his eyes. *To be free like that,* he thought. Free of pain, free of his heart. But even as he thought it he knew it was impossible.

He wasn't a bird. Not an animal. He was a human being with feelings and a need for love, for companionship.

The seagull disappeared from view, and Devon pushed himself off the rocks. *Where's the answer—where?* he asked himself. Confused and lonely, he climbed onto his motorcycle and headed back to Nan's.

Chapter 4

It was Friday evening, the day before Elizabeth's Project Adventure trip was to start. Elizabeth pulled the duffel bag she'd bought at the Natural High Sporting Goods store onto her neatly made bed and pulled out the list she'd made of things she'd need for her camping trip. Looking at the paper, she could hardly believe how little stuff she was going to be getting by on for a whole week—one change of clothes, a sleeping bag, a pocketknife, a compass, a folding tin cup and pail, a tin plate, a fork and knife, a toothbrush, and a small tube of toothpaste.

She opened her dresser drawer and glanced at herself in the mirror. *Am I really going to do this?* she asked herself, feeling a thrill of excitement mingled with anxiety. She took a deep breath and reminded herself that she had to pack.

As she folded her clothes and placed them in

the duffel bag, she recalled how in the past no matter where she was going, she had always packed some memento of Todd. A picture or some tiny gift he'd given her.

She zipped the bag and plopped down on the bed beside it, feeling a pinch of sorrow. The week had been so lonely . . . and so long. No Todd, no Devon—just a lonesome ache in her heart.

She felt herself falling into a depression and pushed herself off the bed. *Snap out of it!* she ordered herself. She should be feeling excited, not sad. She was about to leave the whole mess behind. This Project Adventure trip was about Elizabeth Wakefield on her own. Maybe if she had some time to herself, she could figure out who she really wanted to be with—Devon or Todd. Because even though she was angry with both of them, she knew that sooner or later she was going to have to choose. She couldn't stay angry forever.

But now wasn't the time to think about that. Now she needed to pack.

She was reaching beside her bed for the tiny bag of camping accessories she'd picked up at Natural High when Jessica burst into the room, carrying a shopping bag filled to the brim. She was dressed to kill in a scoop-neck yellow tank top and skintight designer jeans with high-heeled patent leather sandals. Her toenails matched the tank top.

"Here, I thought you could use a few things," she said, emptying the shopping bag onto Elizabeth's bed.

Elizabeth stared at the array of beauty products in amazement. There were facial masks and microbead cleansers, eye creams, hand creams, face creams, and foot creams. There were toners and astringents, shampoos and conditioners, hair sprays, mousses, and gels.

"What's all this?" Elizabeth asked, baffled.

"I couldn't very well let you run off to the wilderness without something to protect your hair and skin, now could I?" Jessica asked incredulously. "It's bad enough you're doing this crazy thing in the first place."

Elizabeth smiled in spite of herself. Only Jessica would think to take a cosmetic counter's worth of beauty aids on a wilderness survival trip. "Thanks anyway," Elizabeth said, her smile fading as she recalled *why* she was going on the trip. "But I have all I need right here." She patted the duffel bag.

Jessica peeked into the bag and guffawed. "That's *it*?" she squealed. "Omigosh! A pair of jeans, two sweatshirts, and a week's worth of socks and *underwear*?" She covered her mouth to hold in a laugh. "Lucky for you all you'll be running into are some *bears!*"

"I'm going on this trip to learn how to survive in the wilderness, not to pick up guys," Elizabeth reminded her. "Like I have any interest in that right now *anyway*," she added pointedly.

Jessica plopped on the bed, digging a heel into

Elizabeth's spotlessly clean cream-colored rug. "The reason I came in here," she said, apparently choosing to ignore Elizabeth's remark, "is to ask you if you'd *please* help me with the party invitations. Otherwise I'll have to settle for something written by Lila or me, and it'll be just awful."

Elizabeth frowned. The last thing she wanted to do was think about a party. "It won't be awful if you do it," she said. "You write as well as I do, and Lila's not illiterate."

Jessica heaved an exasperated breath. "Lila will be too busy with the decorations and setup," she said. "*Please?* I promise I'll never ask you for anything again."

Elizabeth sighed. She was going off on this trip to pull herself together, to clear up her thinking and get in touch with her emotions. It probably wasn't a good idea to go there harboring grudges. What harm would it do for her to write something short and sweet for Jessica's party? "Oh, all right," she said. "I'll put something together tonight before I leave in the morning so you can get it copied." She zipped her duffel bag and stowed it under the bed. "And I'll be back next Saturday morning to help with the preparations, OK?"

"Thanks, Liz!" Jessica said, giving Elizabeth's arm a squeeze.

"Well, here it is," Keith said to Todd, pulling a battered but still serviceable mountain bike off the bike rack of his car Friday afternoon. They were at the base of one of the mountains that surrounded Sweet Valley. Earlier that afternoon during lunch Todd had run into Keith on the ramp outside the cafeteria and had mentioned that he might like to try biking. Keith had told Todd to meet the group three miles south of the Great Mountain Reserve, on Mountain Road, at five if he was serious. So far Todd and Keith were the only ones there.

Todd checked out the bike Keith had brought him, climbing on to get a feel for the suspension. "Feels pretty good," he told Keith, testing the steering. "So where's the rest of the crew?"

Before Keith could answer, a souped-up VW van pulled up and three guys piled out. "Here they are now," Keith said, holding up a hand in greeting. "How goes it, brother bikers?" he called to his friends.

"Hey, Keith!" a couple of the guys called back. The third one, a guy with long black hair and Native American features, raised his hand in greeting. Although the three guys were hippie types like Keith—with bandannas, tie-dyed T-shirts, and grungy cutoff jeans—as they pulled their mountain bikes from the van Todd couldn't help noticing that they weren't the muscleless, pasty-faced moon watchers he'd expected. Their skin was tan, and their leg muscles bulged like professional wrestlers'. *From mountain biking?* Todd wondered.

Once all the bikes were out of the van, Keith said, "C'mere, guys, I want you to meet my buddy Todd."

"Hey, guys," Todd said with a tentative smile.

"This is Moonraker," Keith told Todd, indicating a guy with wavy copper hair who was wearing a red, white, and blue bandanna. "Pleased to meet you," Moonraker said, extending his hand.

"Likewise," Todd replied, shaking it.

"I'm Johnny D.," a big guy with blond hair and a thick mustache said.

Todd shook Johnny D.'s hand, impressed by the strength of his grip.

"Johnny worked with Whale Save for three years up in Alaska," Keith explained. "He can lift a five-hundred-pound anchor with his bare hands."

Johnny smiled good-naturedly. "Maybe a three-hundred-pounder," he amended, slapping Keith on the back.

"And the quiet one here," Keith summed up, chucking his chin at the guy with long black hair, "is Drew Black Bear. He's into nature. He can tell you what the trees are thinking, man."

Drew nodded to Todd.

Once the introductions were completed, Keith said, "Time to do some riding!"

Everyone jumped on their bikes and headed for the mountain trail. As Todd followed the group he glanced up at the surrounding mountains, taking a deep breath of air filled with the aroma of pine trees and wildflowers. *Just being out in nature makes you feel better,* Todd decided as the group reached the trail that would take them to the top of the mountain.

This isn't so hard, he thought as they began their trek up the incline, whizzing past trees as their bikes bounced along the rocky trail.

But before long, Todd's bike had begun to move more and more slowly. Besides the brutal toll on his legs there were downed branches on the trail to contend with and potholes to avoid. Todd realized that what he had thought was going to be a breeze after all his basketball training was turning out to be tougher than he had imagined.

By the time they were halfway up the mountain, Todd was sweating buckets and panting like he'd run a marathon. *There isn't enough water in Sweet Valley to cool me down,* he thought, reaching for his water bottle.

He was beginning to wonder if he was going to make it all the way when suddenly there was a clearing, and he could see the top of the mountain. "Almost there, men!" Moonraker called out.

Todd reached deep down in his reserves, straining to make it to the top of the mountain. *A few more feet,* he told himself. *Just a few more.* His leg muscles strained, and his heart felt like it was going to burst. And then suddenly he was there, staring across a vista of emerald green mountains surrounded by blue sky and pure white clouds. It was like discovering a new world—a place where no human being had ever laid foot before. The rush of adrenaline was incredible!

"Unreal!" Todd exclaimed, slapping Keith five as the group climbed off their bikes to check out the valley below.

Todd joined them, his legs wobbling from exertion. "That was amazing," he said, pushing against a tree to stretch out his hamstrings.

"Quite a rush, hey?" Johnny D. prompted, handing Todd an energy bar as Todd stepped away from the tree.

"Thanks," Todd said. "Yeah, it's quite a rush, all right." He could actually feel the anger, aggression, and hurt flowing out with his sweat, blasted out of him by the clean mountain air. It sure felt better than beating on Devon.

As the guys climbed back on their bikes to finish the trek down Todd couldn't help thinking this challenge was exactly what he needed.

At 4:30 A.M. on Saturday morning Elizabeth shut off her alarm. Groaning, she stumbled out of bed. After splashing some cold water on her face and brushing her teeth, she dressed in jeans, a T-shirt, and hiking boots; grabbed her duffel bag from underneath her bed; and went downstairs to wait for the Project Adventure van to arrive.

The sun had barely touched the horizon when the van drove up to her house. Elizabeth waved to the driver from the doorstep so he wouldn't honk the horn and wake the neighborhood. Then she hurried to climb in as someone opened the van's sliding door from inside.

Besides the two guides, Gary and Kate (who, Elizabeth noticed, were wearing Project Adventure T-shirts and name tags), there were three women and an older man sitting in the van. "Hey," a woman with short blond hair and a pretty smile said as Elizabeth climbed in. She stuck out her hand. "I'm Dory, here for the challenge." She laughed.

Elizabeth smiled politely. "Elizabeth Wakefield," she said, wondering if she was supposed to add more. She really didn't feel like talking about Todd and Devon.

No sooner had Elizabeth settled into her seat than the rest of the group began to introduce themselves.

"I'm Margaret," a slightly overweight woman said. "I'm a housewife, here to cope with middle age," she told Elizabeth with a grin.

Elizabeth smiled and shook her hand.

"My name's Ginny," a pretty woman with chin-length, ginger-colored hair and a cute figure told her. "Since we seem to be confessing our reasons for coming on this trip," she said, glancing playfully around the group, "I'll tell you that—number one—I was divorced a couple of months ago, and—number two—I need to prove to myself that I can take care of myself and my

59

two boys. The kids are with my mother for the week."

Finally there was Matt, the older man. "Ever since I was a kid," Matt told Elizabeth after introducing himself, "I wanted to see what Daniel Boone went through. Now that I'm retired, I figured it was time to find out."

"So what's your story?" Dory asked. Dory, who seemed to be in her early twenties, had obviously already taken on a leadership role in the group.

Elizabeth smiled. "I just needed a break from school," she said, polite but reserved. For her the trip was about giving herself time to think. Time away from the real world for some honest reflection. She didn't feel comfortable discussing it with strangers, as nice as they seemed to be.

The group chatted amiably as they made their way to the Great Mountain National Reserve. But Elizabeth kept her eyes on the scenery unfolding outside. As they drove deeper and deeper into the woods she felt a thrill of anticipation. It was a true wilderness, unsettled and untamed.

The van came to a stop in the middle of nowhere, and the driver helped them unload their sleeping gear and duffel bags. "You're on your own now," he told the group once the van was empty. Then he closed the sliding door and took off back down the mountain, leaving the Project Adventure members alone with the trees and sky and sounds of nature.

Once the van had disappeared from sight, Gary—a nice-looking guy with an athletic build, tan skin, and brownish blond hair—clapped to get the group's attention. "OK, group, first thing we have to do is find a spot to set up camp," he told them. "Lesson number one—what should we look for in a camping spot?" He glanced around the group. "Anyone?"

Dory spoke up first. "A place near water?"

Gary nodded. "Good. Yes, we want to find a water source before we set up our camp. Anything else?"

"Shelter from the elements!" Matt called out.

"Good," Gary said. "What else?"

Elizabeth thought about it. What would make a good campsite? "Someplace you're not likely to be attacked by wild animals?" she asked tentatively, recalling what her mother had said about being mauled by bears.

"Excellent!" Gary said. "Yes. Animals have their spaces just like human beings. Territories, we call them. You want to make sure you're not encroaching on any dangerous animal's territory before setting up camp."

"How do we make sure of that?" Margaret asked dubiously.

"I'll let our wildlife expert, Kate, explain that," Gary told her, stepping aside for Kate to take center stage. Kate, like Gary, was athletically built and very tan, with stunning green eyes and short-cropped brown hair. *Cute, but definitely knows*

61

how to take care of herself, Elizabeth decided.

"OK, campers," Kate said, smiling at the group. "Here's the story. Animals—*all* animals, including human beings—leave trails. Now, those trails can be in the form of tracks, broken branches, droppings, or claw marks on trees—which, by the way, both bears and mountain lions leave when they sharpen their claws."

"Omigosh!" Ginny gasped.

Kate smiled benignly. "Don't panic," she said, and the rest of the group laughed nervously. "As Gary mentioned, animals keep to their territories. A bear or a mountain lion will use the same 'scratching post' every time it sharpens its claws. Once you spot its tree, you can steer around it and you'll be relatively safe from running into the owner. Remember, most animals—even predators—are as wary of us as we are of them. Just please stay clear of mothers with their young. A mother animal can become quite savage when protecting her babies. Just like human mothers."

Elizabeth was amazed. They just jumped right into it, didn't they? The group hadn't been here ten minutes, and already they'd learned practically all there was to know about picking out a campsite.

"OK, gang," Gary said, interrupting her thoughts. "Let's break into two groups and find some water!"

As Elizabeth joined Matt, Ginny, and Kate her

heart pounded with a strange mixture of excitement and fear at what the coming week might hold.

"So basically I told her we couldn't write the invitation without her," Jessica concluded as she and Lila walked into the Valley Mall.

"I've got to hand it to you, Jess," Lila said as they made their way to the escalator. "I didn't think you could do it."

"Have a little faith!" Jessica said with a laugh. She and Lila rode the escalator to the second floor, then headed for the Paper Tiger. They had all the tableware they needed, but they still had to pick up lanterns for around the lake and citronella candles for the tables to keep away the mosquitoes.

"I still can't believe Liz went off on that goofy adventure," Jessica commented incredulously as she and Lila made their way through the crowds of shoppers. "She didn't even take a lipstick with her! Of course," she continued, checking out her crop top and black shorts in one of the shop windows, "if I didn't plan the parties in the Wakefield family, there wouldn't be any."

"That's for sure," Lila agreed. Suddenly she grabbed Jessica's arm. "Ooo, isn't that just *stunning?*" she gasped, coming to a stop in front of Lisette's, a very expensive boutique that specialized in imported clothes. In the window was a lovely camel pantsuit with black trim, a Nadine original.

Lila caught sight of her reflection and grimaced. "It makes this outfit look like a Salvation Army special," she moaned.

Jessica laughed, looking over Lila's blue linen dress. "Your Lorenzo Fabrini *original?* Only if the Salvation Army is on Rodeo Drive."

"Oh, I just *have* to have it," Lila said desperately.

"Didn't we come here for party accessories?" Jessica reminded her, raising an eyebrow.

"Come on," Lila cajoled, pulling Jessica into the boutique. "It will only take a second, I promise."

Forty-five minutes later Jessica and Lila left Lisette's, loaded with packages. There was Lila's new outfit plus a new purse, new shoes, new stockings, a lovely beaded necklace and matching earrings, and a hat to go with it.

"Now, can we *please* get on with the *party* shopping?" Jessica whined as they stumbled out of the store.

Lila rolled her eyes. "I didn't take *that* long," she retorted.

"Not much," Jessica said, but she didn't push it. She needed Lila's help, and getting into an argument now was probably not a good idea. "Could you hold this for a second?" she asked, loading the hatbox into one of Lila's shopping bags. She pulled a party list and a pen out of her purse. "OK, let's go over what we've got."

"Shoot," Lila prompted her.

"Invitations?"

"Check," Lila said, and Jessica crossed it off the list.

"Band?" Jessica continued.

"Check," Lila responded, resting her packages on a bench.

"Beverages?" Jessica read.

"Check."

"Charcoal?" Jessica continued.

"Not me," Lila announced.

Jessica looked at her in exasperation. "You didn't get the charcoal?"

Lila looked annoyed. "You didn't *ask* me to get it, so why *would* I get it?"

"But I was sure . . . ," Jessica said, tapping the top of the pen against her lips.

"And how was I supposed to carry it anyway?" Lila added. "We need at least thirty pounds of the stuff."

Jessica's jaw dropped. "That *much?*"

"Well, how many grills have we got?" Lila asked. "We can't cook all those ribs on one grill."

"Grills?" Jessica repeated weakly.

Lila gave her an incredulous look. "Jessica, you did ask some of our group to lend us grills, didn't you?" she demanded.

Jessica shrugged. "I hadn't thought about it," she said helplessly.

Lila plopped down beside her packages. "And I don't suppose you figured out how we're going to carry all that stuff to the lake and set it up either," she said flatly.

Jessica shook her head. "Why didn't you mention all this before?"

Lila rolled her eyes. "I thought you had it all taken care of."

Jessica sat down beside Lila. "And after this shopping spree of yours we don't even have enough arms to carry the lanterns out of the mall, never mind thirty pounds of charcoal and a busload of grills," she said with a hint of irritation.

Lila scowled. "Don't blame *me*," she responded angrily. "I did everything you asked me to do. Remember, this is *your* party, not mine."

Jessica crossed her arms over her chest in frustration. "Great," she said. "Less than a week till the party, and all we've got is some raw honey Dijon ribs and a bunch of throwaway dinnerware."

Lila pulled her new shoes out of the bag. "Aren't these just *fabulous*?" she gushed, examining her new Italian leather sandals.

"Lila!" Jessica interjected. "I've got more important things on my mind than your shoes. We need some guys to do the heavy work."

Lila frowned. "Aren't *we* touchy," she said.

Jessica ignored her. "And some *girls* to help with the organization," she added. She stared at her feet a minute, then snapped her fingers. "I've got it!" she exclaimed. "Call everyone you know and tell them to meet us at a party-planning pow-wow at the Dairi Burger after school on Monday. We're going to get this bar-b-cue under way!"

Chapter 5

Todd was in the locker room Monday after basketball practice, getting ready to go on another biking session, when it dawned on him that he hadn't seen Elizabeth since Friday. *Where's she been hiding anyway?* he wondered. Funny, he hadn't really thought about that until now. Naturally he still missed her like crazy. But somehow releasing his hurt and grief had made missing her easier to bear.

There really was something to riding hard, he'd discovered. Something about being out in the wild with the trees and mountains and sky. Afterward the guys just sat around and chilled—told jokes they couldn't tell their girlfriends; talked about sports, about making it in the world, about things girls seemed to have trouble understanding—like a guy's need for freedom which doesn't mean you don't *love* your girlfriend, just that you need your own space sometimes too.

So maybe he had more space than he wanted right now. Begging Elizabeth to come back hadn't worked. Maybe the best way to win her back was to make himself scarce. Yeah, let her wonder where *he* was for a change.

He pulled on a pair of khaki shorts and a white T-shirt, then laced up his hiking boots. "Hey, Wilkins," Tom Hacket called from across the locker room, "you hiking or driving to Dairi Burger today?" Tom was a guard on the SVH basketball team and a friend of Todd's.

Todd smiled wryly. "Sorry, Hacket," he said. "I've got other plans."

"Yeah? You ditched us yesterday too," Aaron reminded him. "What's the story?"

Todd glanced at Aaron, who had just come in from soccer practice. "I've got a new hobby," Todd said, slicking back his hair, which was still wet from the shower.

"Who is she?" asked Paul Isaacs, one of the seniors on the team.

Tom shot Paul a withering look.

"What'd I do?" Paul asked, throwing his hands in the air, apparently missing the point that the last thing Todd needed right now was another girl in his life.

"I'm talking about a sport, Paul," Todd answered. "I've started mountain biking with Keith and some of his buddies."

"*Mountain* biking!" Aaron said with a surprised

grin. "You mean like bonding with nature?"

"Ooo," teased Jason Mann, one of Paul's classmates. "How *California.*"

"OK, OK, you guys," Todd said. "So mountain biking's got a rep as a trendy sport. The fact is, it's really hard work pushing a bike up a mountain. A lot harder than scrambling around a basketball court."

"Is that a fact?" Tom Hacket said in a challenging voice.

Todd shrugged. "Hey, I'm as into basketball as a guy can get," he told Tom, "but mountain biking is tough. I mean, it really pushes your limits. And there's something cool about being in the fresh air and sunshine, just you and the road. You can't beat the high you get reaching the top of the mountain."

Aaron looked interested. "You know, it does sound kind of intriguing," he said. "I mean, it must take some pretty strong legs."

Paul slapped his thigh muscles. "So does running around a basketball court," he pointed out.

Tom grinned. "I'm with you, Paul," he said. "I'll take a burger over biking any day."

"Count me in with the burger crowd," Jason chimed in. The three guys started for the door, and Tom turned around as Paul opened it. "You coming, Aaron?"

Aaron looked from the guys to Todd. "Any room on that mountain for me?" he asked.

"Sure," Todd said, slapping on some aftershave. "The more the merrier."

Aaron shrugged in Tom's direction. "I think I'm gonna give it a try," he said.

Tom shook his head as if the two of them were crazy, then he moved toward the door. "Have fun, girls," he called. The other guys laughed as they stepped out of the locker room.

"Don't choke on a burger on my account," Aaron yelled as the door closed behind them.

Todd grinned at Aaron. "Guess it's just you and me, buddy," he said.

As they left the gym Winston, who was watching Bruce and Barry on the tennis court, noticed them and jogged over. "Headed to the Dairi Burger?" Winston asked.

"We're going mountain biking," Aaron told him. "Workout high."

"Workout high, huh?" Barry asked, shouldering his racket as he sauntered over.

"I think I've heard about that," Winston joked.

"You guys wanna come?" Todd asked.

Barry looked at Winston, who grinned right back. "I'm in if you are," Barry said.

"I'll try anything once," Winston replied.

"Hey, Bruce!" Aaron yelled. "Come here for a minute! I got a proposition for you."

Todd grinned. This was more like it. A bunch of guys, the mountains, and good times. He was beginning to feel better already.

❖   ❖   ❖

"I think we should hang the lanterns on the lake *and* in the trees," Amy suggested. "That'll look pretty from the road." Jessica, Lila, Amy, and Maria Santelli were at the Dairi Burger Monday afternoon, discussing the Secca Lake party as they waited for the guys to get there.

"We can't put lights in the trees, Amy," Jessica said. "They're electric, and our cords won't reach that far."

"Bummer," Amy said, resting her chin in her hands.

"It'll look cool enough with the lanterns just reflecting off the water," Maria consoled her, taking a sip of her chocolate shake.

"Right," Lila agreed, straightening the sleeves of her new Nadine outfit. "It's not Christmas anyway, Amy."

"You don't only put lights in trees for Christmas," Amy said haughtily. "Right, Jess?"

Jessica stabbed a french fry into some ketchup. "Never mind Christmas," she complained. "It's not even going to be a *party* if we don't get the guys to help us." She looked impatiently toward the door. "Where are they?" she demanded, turning back to the table. "They were supposed to be here ages ago." She glared at her friends. "*I* called Bruce. Didn't any of *you* bother to call any of the guys?"

Lila gave her an annoyed look. "I most certainly did," she told Jessica. "I called Aaron."

"And I talked to Barry," Amy defended herself.

71

Maria popped one of Jessica's french fries into her mouth, then caught the other three girls glaring at her. "What?" she said. "*Naturally* I mentioned it to Winston."

Jessica looked baffled. "And they all said they'd be here?"

"Yep," Lila told her.

"Barry did," Amy replied.

"You're talking Winston," Maria reminded her, pulling a napkin out of the holder to wipe ketchup off her fingers. "Of course he said he'd be here."

"Then where *are* they?" Jessica demanded. She angrily blew a strand of hair out of her eyes. "Don't they know an opportunity to hang out with the coolest girls in school when they see it?"

"You've got a point there, Jess," Lila agreed, checking her manicure. "It's totally bizarre."

"It isn't that unusual," Maria disagreed. "They're guys, after all. Why don't we call them again and see what they're doing? Maybe they just forgot."

"All four of them?" Amy asked incredulously.

"Like I said," Maria reiterated, "they're guys."

Lila pulled a gold compact from her purse and reapplied her lipstick. "True. Maybe we *should* call them."

Jessica looked relieved. "Of course," she said, pushing away her plate of french fries. "We should have reminded them at lunch that we were having this meeting."

"Um, guys?" Amy said with a skeptical look on her face. "I *did* remind Barry."

Lila glanced at Jessica. "Maybe Barry forgot twice?" she offered weakly.

Jessica slapped her palms on the table. "That's it," she said. "Pull out your cell phones. We're gonna make some calls."

The girls fumbled in their purses for their phones and began to punch in numbers. One after the other they shook their heads.

"Barry isn't home," Amy said.

"Neither is Winston," Maria told the group.

"Aaron's out. His mom doesn't know where," Lila informed them.

"Take a guess about Bruce," Jessica said, sticking her phone back in her purse. She squinted thoughtfully and tapped her chin. "Not one of them is home, and no one seems to know where any of them are," she said. "Now, what do you suppose that means?"

Amy finished her soda. "That they're up to something?" she suggested.

Jessica nodded. "I'd say," she answered. "The question is, what?"

The sun was sinking lower on the horizon as Elizabeth—following a set of squirrel tracks—pushed her way through some brambles into a clearing beneath an oak tree. After being prepped by Kate and Gary the group had split up and gone out on their own for the first time.

"I want you to really study your surroundings," Kate had told them before they left the campsite. "Look for animal tracks and edible plants, get a feel for your surroundings. We'll all meet back here at dusk and discuss what you've found," she had added. "Gary and I will answer any questions you may have then."

Off on her own, Elizabeth was surprised at how quiet it was. Except for the chirping of birds and the wind rustling through the trees, there wasn't a sound—no cars, no mowers, no children playing. Just her and the woods.

She took a deep breath of pine-scented air, then picked up a half-eaten acorn she spied lying on the ground. From the way it was nibbled, she tried to determine if the tracks she was following were made by a red or a gray squirrel.

The red squirrel was smaller than the gray, she'd learned, so the nibbles would be smaller. She examined the tooth marks carefully and decided the acorn had been a red squirrel's meal.

With a satisfied smile Elizabeth dropped the acorn and sat on a nearby log. A few days into her adventure, she was tired but exhilarated. She'd learned so much since coming here, like how to tell if a plant was edible or not. She'd thought it was just something someone told you, but now she knew how to tell even if she'd never seen or heard of the plant before.

Gary had told them that first you had to make sure the plant wasn't a contact poison. The way you did that was to rub the leaf or sap of the plant over your wrist and wait fifteen minutes, looking for signs of redness, itching, or blistering. That seemed simple enough. But after that, there was a long process of tests and waiting for the results of the tests, before one could finally eat the plant.

"Of course, by that time I'd probably be dead of starvation," Elizabeth mumbled. It seemed much easier to simply search for foods she could easily identify.

Luckily, since the group was only going to be on their own for a week, Gary had also pointed out some edible plants. The roots of young ferns were good, Elizabeth had learned, and of course there were nuts from limber and sugar pines. "Always avoid mushrooms," Gary had told them. One tiny swallow of certain mushrooms could be fatal.

As Elizabeth went over her survival tips she suddenly realized she'd forgotten about Todd and Devon for the moment. *Funny,* she thought, *I haven't been thinking about the guys much, even though they're the reason I'm here.*

She realized she was starting to feel more attuned to her surroundings, more aware. And she was honing her observational skills—not a bad thing for an aspiring journalist. *Which reminds me,* she thought, *I'm supposed to be tracking squirrels.*

She pushed herself up from the log and studied the ground. The squirrel tracks led to a huge pine tree straight ahead. Quietly Elizabeth crept toward the pine. As she drew closer she heard soft chattering coming from a hollow in the tree. *Gotcha!* she thought excitedly.

She crept closer to the tree and quietly peeked inside the hollow. To her surprise she discovered two red squirrels, although she'd seen only one set of tracks. *Maybe one of them was waiting here for its mate to bring home supper,* she thought, delighted.

But the delight quickly faded as she watched the two squirrels cuddling together in the small hollow. Suddenly her loneliness and estrangement from both Todd and Devon came racing back to her. She slumped against the tree. *What am I going to do? Can I live without them? And if not, how can I ever choose one of them above the other?* she wondered hopelessly.

For a moment she felt overwhelmed, unable to even move. She took a deep breath. *You can do it, Liz,* she told herself. *You've got almost an entire week left to make a decision. An entire week to figure out your life.*

She only hoped it was enough time.

"Hey, Todd, how's it goin'?" Aaron called from his locker when Todd walked into school Tuesday morning.

"Great," Todd answered, joining him near

the wall. "How's everything with you?"

Aaron gave Todd the A-OK sign. "Still smelling that sweet mountain air," Aaron said with a grin as Winston sauntered up to the lockers.

"Was that cool or what?" Winston enthused.

Aaron patted his thighs. "That workout is going to be *great* for my soccer game." He glanced down the hall. "Hey, there's Keith. How's it goin', man?" he called, waving Keith their way.

"Hey, guys!" Keith called back. He pulled some books from his locker, then joined the group. "Still feeling the high?" he asked them with a grin.

"That's for sure," Todd said. "You guys are planning to go again tonight, right?"

"Every night," Keith told him.

"I'll be there," Todd said. He glanced around the group. "Any of you guys want to join me?"

"I'm in," Winston said.

"Count on me," Aaron concurred.

"And I'm definitely going on that big weekend ride at the Great Mountain National Reserve," Todd added. Yesterday Keith had mentioned that the bikers were planning a major ride at the Reserve Friday night. "The mountains at the Reserve are *real* mountains," he'd told the group. "It's the difference between hopping a picket fence and scaling the Great Wall of China."

The other guys said they were definitely in on it too. "I'm taking my bike for a tune-up tonight," Winston joked.

Keith laughed. "Cool," he said. "This weekend should be a real trip."

Just then Aaron nudged Todd. "Look who's here," he said.

Todd looked up. Devon was walking down the other end of the hall. Funny, Todd would have expected to see red when he caught sight of Devon again. But the anger he felt for Devon had diminished a lot, as if his brain was tired of holding on to it. Right now he was more concerned with seeing Elizabeth. Where was she? He hadn't seen her all day.

Keith glanced down the hall. "Is that the dude who muscled in on Elizabeth?" he asked.

Todd nodded. "Yeah, that's him, all right."

"You know, maybe we should ask him along on one of our outings," Keith suggested.

Aaron looked at Keith as if he were crazy. "Are you serious? After what he did to Todd?"

Keith ignored him. "You still mad at him, man?" he asked Todd.

Todd shrugged. "Not as much as I was. But I'm not sure I want to go riding with him."

"You weren't sure you wanted to go riding *period* a couple of days ago," Keith reminded him. "Why don't you give it a shot?"

Todd stared down the hall at Devon. "I don't know, man," he said. "Deciding to go riding is one thing. Deciding to go riding with the guy who stole Liz is another."

Keith raised his eyebrows. "The guy who *stole*

her? You don't think maybe Liz had something to do with it, do you, bro? I mean, from what I know of Elizabeth Wakefield, she's not some wimpy chick, man. I don't think that Devon guy so much *stole* her as she decided she wanted to start *seeing* him."

"Hey!" Aaron said, ready to defend Todd.

But Todd held up a hand, stopping Aaron. Maybe Keith was right. It was true that Devon had fallen for Elizabeth, but when it came right down to it, Elizabeth had done what she wanted to do. He supposed it wasn't his fault *or* Devon's. Besides, being ticked at Devon wasn't going to help him win Elizabeth back. "You make a good point," he told Keith, keeping his eyes on Devon.

Keith punched Todd lightly on the biceps. "Right on, man," he said.

Devon was pulling his history book from his locker when he noticed that Wilkins guy coming after him. Tensing up, he shoved the book back into his locker and got ready for another brawl. "Back for more?" he challenged as Todd approached his locker.

Todd shook his head. "I'm not here to fight, Devon," he said calmly.

Yeah? Devon thought. *Then what* do *you want?* "If you want to know where Liz is," he said curtly, "I haven't seen her."

"Actually," Todd said. "I'm here to apologize."

Devon was taken off guard—but only for a

moment. His surprise was soon clouded by suspicion. "Yeah, right," he said sarcastically. "Come off it. What do you *really* want, Wilkins?"

"You want to know the truth?" Todd asked, leaning against a locker.

Devon crossed his arms over his chest. "That would be nice for a change," he said bitterly.

"I came to invite you to something," Todd told him.

Devon stared at him in disbelief. Was this guy for real? "Invite me to *what?*" he asked. "A duel?"

Todd smiled. "Not today," he replied, scratching the back of his head. He sighed. "Look, I know we got off on the wrong foot—"

"To say the least," Devon muttered.

"But I'm really not the type to jump to conclusions about people," Todd continued, ignoring Devon's remark. "And I'd like a chance to get to know you better."

Devon gave him an incredulous look. *Am I hearing right?* he wondered. *What is Wilkins talking about?*

Todd apparently noticed Devon's surprise. "I know this sounds like it's coming out of nowhere," he said, "but the truth is, I've been thinking a lot about what happened, and I realize that Elizabeth followed her own path. No one forced her decision. I was just angry and hurt, and I wasn't looking at the situation clearly."

Devon felt the hairs prickle at the back of his neck. *Is Todd suggesting that I'm angry and hurt?* Devon wondered. *Is that what that remark meant?*

Devon closed his locker, wondering if his feelings showed that much on his face.

"Anyway," Todd continued. "Some of the guys and I have been going mountain biking after school. It's really awesome. I mean, you'd be amazed at the release it gives you—how it puts things in perspective."

Devon snorted. So that's what this bozo was talking about. Mountain biking. Right. "How hip," he said sarcastically.

Todd frowned. "That's not what it's about," he said. "It's getting in touch with yourself, sweating out your problems. . . ."

Yeah, right, Devon thought. As far as *he* was concerned, what Todd and his pals were doing had less to do with getting in touch with themselves than being an excuse for a boys' night out. He rolled his eyes as Todd continued telling him about the natural high it gave him, the camaraderie with his fellow bikers. *Maybe it's OK for a California jock,* Devon decided, *but not for me.*

"So what do you say?" Todd asked him. "You want to join us?"

Devon looked at him for a minute, then smiled caustically. "Thanks, but no thanks," he said bitterly. "I've got better things to do with my time."

Todd shrugged. "Hey, if that's the way you want it," he said. "But if you change your mind, you know where to find me."

"Right," Devon said coldly, then he turned and walked the other way.

Chapter 6

"Well, look who's here," Jessica said to Lila, Amy, and Maria Santelli as they made their way to their usual table in the cafeteria Tuesday afternoon. Waiting for them there were Bruce, Barry, Aaron, and Winston. "Long time no see," Jessica quipped sarcastically as she sat down next to Aaron.

"Hey, girls," Winston said with a silly wave.

"Don't 'hey, girls' us," Maria shot back, shoving her lunch tray between Winston's and Aaron's. "Where were you yesterday?"

"We're not used to being kept waiting," Lila said, wiping some crumbs off her seat with a paper napkin.

The guys glanced at each other but didn't answer. "Would someone pass the salt?" Bruce requested as the rest of the guys became superinterested in their lunches.

Jessica blew out a mouthful of air, exasperated. She pushed the saltshaker across the table toward Bruce. *What is it with these guys?* she wondered. *It's like pulling teeth to get a straight answer from any of them.* "Well?" she said, impatiently tapping her foot. "We're waiting."

Winston glanced at Bruce and made a weird spinning motion with his hand. The other guys laughed.

Are they calling me crazy? Jessica wondered, irked. "Maybe you've forgotten about the Secca Lake party this weekend," she said angrily. "But if we girls have to plan this all by ourselves, the least you can do is show up."

Aaron forced the smile off his face, replacing it with a serious look. "We're sorry we missed the meeting yesterday," he said, "but we promise we'll be at the party on Saturday. Right, guys?"

"Count me in," Winston said, taking Maria's hand. "You know how I feel about cheerleaders."

The girls laughed.

"After all," Bruce added with a sexy grin, "we wouldn't want to miss dancing with the most beautiful girls in Sweet Valley."

Jessica's anger faded at the compliment. Bruce's attempt at being charming was as phony as the rest of him, but at least he was trying to be nice for a change. *This is more like it,* she decided as Barry kissed Amy's hand. Suddenly she felt a whole lot better. "I've got a great idea!" she said, slapping her palms on the table. "How about we all get together later just for fun? Get a pizza at Guido's or something."

She might as well have told the guys there was a huge surprise math exam tomorrow. They suddenly became quiet, their gazes locked on the table. Jessica glanced at Lila and the other girls in total confusion.

"Hey, where's Elizabeth these days?" Aaron asked, changing the subject. "I haven't seen her in a while."

"Yeah," Barry joined in, obviously relieved to be talking about something besides meeting the girls after school. "Where *is* Elizabeth? She hasn't been in English all week."

"Elizabeth?" Lila repeated, straightening the gold chain around her neck. "Oh, she's off bonding with Mom Nature."

"Yeah, she's playing cavewoman," Jessica joked, momentarily forgetting about the pizza.

"Cavewoman?" Bruce repeated, suddenly becoming interested in the conversation.

Jessica grinned. *Maybe meeting a cavewoman is a romantic fantasy of his,* she thought, stifling a laugh. "That's right," she told Bruce. "She's off on this totally nutso mission, learning how to survive in the wilderness on roots and berries."

"Without so much as a cell phone or a nail file," Lila added, shaking her head in amazement.

But the guys didn't seem to think it was so

funny. They exchanged those weird glances they'd been giving each other ever since the girls had joined them.

"I think that's pretty cool—getting in touch with nature," Bruce said.

Jessica's jaw dropped open. She couldn't believe her ears. I'm-too-cool-for-words Patman was turning into Mr. Sensitive? She glanced at the other girls, who seemed just as surprised as she was. *Just what have these guys been putting in their water bottles anyway?* she wondered as she took a bite of her tuna sandwich.

The woods were quiet except for the soothing chirping of crickets and the soft crackle of the campfire glowing beneath the stars. The Project Adventure group had just finished a dinner of trout and dandelion greens they'd worked all afternoon gathering and were relaxing in front of a campfire they'd built themselves.

Elizabeth sat back against a log contentedly. It was Tuesday evening—four days since her quest to find herself had begun. Tonight her problems and Sweet Valley seemed very far away.

"Tired?" Dory asked Elizabeth, joining her.

Elizabeth nodded. "This outing has been intense," she said. "I mean, think of all we've learned since we got here!"

"Yeah," Dory agreed, running a hand through her cropped blond hair. "It's amazing, isn't it? Just a few days ago I wouldn't have known the difference between an oak leaf and a pine needle. Now I can tell if it was a rabbit or a skunk nibbling a fern just by looking at the *tooth* marks!"

Matt, who was sitting nearby, laughed knowingly. "Amazing what you see when you know what to look for, isn't it?" he said. His smile softened, and he smoothed his gray hair. "You know, ever since my wife, Betsy, died, I've been figuring there wasn't much for me to live for. The fact is, it wasn't wanting to be like Daniel Boone that sent me here so much as wanting to find out who I was and what direction I should go in. I'd always had Betsy to tell me that before."

Elizabeth stared at Matt in amazement. That's exactly why she was here. Even though they were generations apart, Matt and she were basically experiencing the same feelings. "I know exactly what you mean," she told him, deciding to open up to the group for the first time. "I didn't really come here to get away from school—I came here to get away from some *guys* at school."

Ginny, who had been sitting warming her hands at the fire, drew closer to the three of them. "I couldn't help overhearing," she said. "Guy troubles. I can certainly relate to that," she added soberly. "The first few years of my marriage were like heaven on earth. Then—*boom!*—reality set in." She pounded her right fist into the palm of her left hand. "It seems that while I was playing the perfect wife and mother, my ex-husband was playing around with his secretary."

"That's terrible!" Elizabeth said. "Why bother getting married if you're not going to be faithful?" she wondered aloud.

Ginny nodded. "My sentiments exactly," she said. "That's why I filed for divorce."

"Divorce, guy trouble . . . ," Margaret commented, shaking her head as she joined the group. "It's never simple, is it?" she said.

"It was simple with me and my Betsy," Matt disagreed.

Margaret's expression softened. "Some of us are lucky, Matt. I've got a good man myself. It's just that the spark seems to have gone. The real reason I came on this survival trip is to try to get that spark back in myself so I can get it back in my marriage."

Elizabeth looked from one member of the group to the next as Gary and Kate joined them. Although she'd known the group members only a short time, they'd gone through so much together that she felt like they were old friends.

She took a deep breath. "I have a confession to make," she said, clutching her hands together nervously.

Dory patted her arm. "We're all here for the same reason, Elizabeth—to find ourselves," she said. "You don't have to tell us anything you don't want to."

Elizabeth shook her head. "I don't mind," she said, giving Dory a small smile. "I actually *need* to talk about it, now that I've got it a little better sorted in my head."

Ginny nodded. "It's good to talk things out," she noted. "Helps you to put your problems in perspective. So let it out."

Elizabeth smiled at her. "Thanks," she said. She took another deep breath. "The problem is, there are these two guys I really care for, Todd and Devon."

"*Two* of them." Margaret shook her head. "That *is* a problem."

Elizabeth nodded. "Yeah," she agreed. "Todd and I had been together forever. Then I met Devon, and it was just like . . . well, there was so much *chemistry* between us, you know?"

"I had that kind of chemistry with my Betsy," Matt said nostalgically.

Elizabeth smiled gently. "If only there were just one of *my* guys," she told him. She glanced around the group. "It was confusing to begin with, loving both of them, then the two of them got into this terrible fight over me." She shook her head. "I was furious at them, which is one of the reasons I decided to come on this outing—I couldn't bear to be around either one after that. But the main reason I came on the Project Adventure trip is that I knew I'd *have* to be around them again. I needed to try to figure out which one I should be with. I decided I need to know Elizabeth Wakefield to make that choice."

Dory nodded sympathetically. "It's a hard thing when you're in love with two men," she said. Her brow furrowed. "Have you reached a decision yet?"

Elizabeth shook her head slowly. "No, I haven't," she told Dory. "But I'm beginning to feel better about the whole situation. Right now I can feel the warmth of what I've shared with both of them. Before I was just angry." She noticed members of the group nodding in understanding. "The trouble is," she continued, "I don't know if it's easier to feel good about Todd and Devon now just because I'm *here* and they're *there*. Up here I don't have to deal with all those crazy emotions."

Margaret raised an eyebrow. "It's possible," she said. "There's something about being out in nature that makes your problems seem smaller."

"Sometimes getting to know yourself makes your problems seem smaller too," Ginny added.

Elizabeth nodded. "Maybe it just feels good to be on my own for a change," she suggested. "Maybe it feels good to make my own decisions about my life." She glanced around the group and saw the understanding in their eyes. To be on your own, in control of your own life—funny . . . before today she'd never realized that she really hadn't been.

"That was incredible!" Todd exclaimed as he, Bruce, and Aaron walked their bikes from the woods into the parking lot of the Sweet Valley

Recreation Park on Tuesday evening. He wiped the sweat from his forehead with the back of his hand and grinned at his friends. The three of them had decided to ride longer than the rest of the group and were just finishing up their trek.

"Amen to that," Aaron agreed, swigging down half of the water in his water bottle.

Bruce pulled off his helmet. "I'm starved," he said, smoothing back his hair. "What do you say we go to Guido's for a pizza?"

"Excellent idea," Aaron told him.

"Sounds good to me," Todd agreed.

The guys climbed into their cars and drove to Guido's. Once there they ordered a large pepperoni with cheese and three supersize soft drinks.

"You think one pizza will be enough?" Aaron asked doubtfully.

"We can always order a second if it's not," Todd told him.

Aaron nodded. "Yeah, I guess."

The guys concentrated on their sodas for a couple of seconds. Then Bruce broke the silence. "So, Wilkins," he said, "I hear your ex is off making like a cavewoman."

Todd nearly choked on his drink. "*What?*" he demanded, slamming down his cup.

Aaron glanced at Bruce, then at Todd. "You mean you didn't know?" Aaron asked incredulously.

Todd shook his head in confusion. "No, I haven't seen Liz for days, but I didn't know why."

He glared at Bruce. "And what do you mean, Liz is making like a cavewoman?" he demanded as all the mellow feeling from the evening's workout seemed to fly out the window.

"Hey, man," Bruce said, sitting back and holding up his hands in surrender. "Don't shoot the messenger, OK?"

Todd took a steadying breath. "Sorry," he said, "but this is the first I've heard of it. Where is she? What's she doing?"

Just then the pizza came. Aaron and Bruce each pulled a slice off onto their paper plates, but Todd suddenly didn't feel very hungry. "So?" he prompted after the other two started eating.

"What I heard," Aaron said, swallowing a huge bite of pizza, "is that Elizabeth's off on this Project Adventure survival thing. You know, they go into the mountains and learn to survive off the land."

"Project Adventure!" Todd exclaimed. "I've heard about that. A bunch of weirdos go off by themselves with just a compass and a pocketknife. Something like that, right?"

Bruce shrugged, wiping sauce off his mouth with the back of his hand. "So I hear."

"So where is she?" Todd demanded, his pulse racing. "What if she's in trouble?"

Aaron gave Todd a look. "Calm down, man," he said. "Elizabeth will be all right." He took another slice of pizza. "Besides, we don't know exactly where she is, just that she's somewhere in the Great Mountain National Reserve."

Todd jumped up from the table. *"What?"* he yelled. "That's out in the middle of nowhere! She won't be able to handle it!" He pulled some money out of his pocket and threw it on the table.

"Where are you going?" Bruce demanded.

"To rescue Liz," Todd shot back, starting for the door.

Aaron jumped up and grabbed Todd by the arm. "Hey, man, chill out," he said. "Did it ever occur to you that maybe Liz doesn't *want* to be rescued? Don't lose your cool, all right? If you have to take your frustrations out on something, take them out on the mountain."

Todd looked from Aaron to the door, then reluctantly sat back down. Maybe Aaron was right. Maybe Elizabeth *didn't* want to be rescued, or why would she have gone on such an idiotic trip in the first place?

When he hadn't seen her in school, he'd just figured she was avoiding him. But was she so angry she had decided to hide out in the *woods?*

Whatever her reasoning, it was going to take a lot of hard pedaling to get Todd's mind off *this* piece of news. Not only did he have to worry about what was happening to Elizabeth now, but he also couldn't help wondering how she was going to miss him if she wasn't even around to know he was gone.

*   *   *

Devon sat at a corner booth in the Dairi Burger, eating a cheeseburger and french fries. Despite the bad memories the place held for him, he had decided that he needed to face his demons. The Dairi Burger had been the spot where everything had begun to go wrong in his life once again. He'd dreamed about the place several times since his fight with Todd. Avoiding the Dairi Burger, he realized, had become an obsession with him.

Tonight he'd decided to end that obsession. It was only a restaurant. And coming here and reliving that horrible night couldn't be any worse than having Elizabeth avoid him all week. Besides, in the back of his mind he had been hoping that Elizabeth might be there.

She wasn't. But his stomach had convinced him to stay. Now, just as he took a bite of his burger, Enid Rollins strolled into the restaurant. Devon watched her from the corner of his eye as she glanced around the restaurant. Elizabeth had introduced Devon to Enid before she started hating him, and Enid had seemed nice enough, but he wasn't in the mood for company.

He silently prayed that Enid wouldn't notice him. Slouching down in his seat, Devon picked up a menu to cover his face—but he was too late. Enid had already spotted him.

"Devon?" she called, coming toward him, her clogs clapping against the linoleum floor as she hurried his way. "I thought that was you. Mind if I join you? I just got out of the library and I'm *famished,* but I hate to eat alone." She sat down without waiting for Devon to answer, pushing a stray hair out of her eyes. "Elizabeth and I usually study together," she explained, "but of course she's off on that wilderness survival trip."

Devon dropped the menu he'd picked up, and his jaw tensed. *Did I hear right?* he wondered. *Liz on some wilderness survival adventure?* It was all he could do to keep from reaching across the table, grabbing Enid by the shoulders, and shaking her. All week he'd been tortured, wondering what had happened to Elizabeth, while all along the answer had been staring him right in the face in the form of Enid. "You mean, you know where Elizabeth is?" he asked.

Enid turned red. Flustered, she laid down her menu. "Uh, well, gee . . . I'm not sure . . . ," she stammered, as if she had let something slip that she shouldn't have.

"Enid," Devon said, fighting to control his temper. "I'm dying here. If you know where Liz is, you have to tell me!"

Enid looked unbearably uncomfortable, her face contorted with indecision. "I don't know," she said miserably, drumming her fingers on the tabletop. "I'm not sure Elizabeth wants you or Todd to know where she is."

Devon folded his hands and stretched them across the table in a gesture of desperation.

"Please," he begged. "Just tell me. I promise I won't do anything—I just need to know."

Enid anxiously searched Devon's face for a moment. Then she let out a sigh. "Oh, all right," she said reluctantly. "But this better not go any further than this table."

Devon nodded. "It won't, I promise. Now where is she?"

Enid looked around the Dairi Burger as if to make sure no one was listening. Then she leaned closer to Devon and said, "Liz is off on a Project Adventure trip, learning to survive in the wilderness."

Devon's jaw dropped. "Project Adventure?" he said, his forehead wrinkling in thought. "Isn't that where they learn to fish with their bare hands and live on roots and berries?"

Enid nodded. "It sure is," she said, waving her hand to get the waitress's attention.

Devon stared at her in disbelief. "What is Liz doing with *that* group?" he demanded.

Enid shrugged as the waitress came toward her. "Learning to fish with her hands and survive on roots and berries," she said facetiously. Her look softened. "I'm sorry," she apologized. "I get cranky when I'm hungry." She turned to the waitress. "Burger with lettuce, tomato, and mayo and a side of onion rings," she said.

Once the waitress had gone, Enid faced Devon with her hands folded in front of her. "The truth is,

Elizabeth felt like she needed some time on her own. That she needed to do something that didn't involve you or Todd."

Devon shook his head. It was like some kind of twisted dream. All his life he had run from his disappointments, and now Elizabeth was running from *him*. "So she took off to the mountains on her *own?*" he asked incredulously. "A fragile girl like Liz, out in the woods by herself? Do you know what could *happen* to her?"

Enid looked annoyed. "Liz is *not* fragile, Devon. She knows how to take care of herself. Besides, there are guides with the group," she added. "It's only at the end that they have to do an overnight solo."

Devon's fist slammed the table. "You mean to tell me she's going to be wandering the mountains by herself? At *night?*" he nearly yelled.

Enid blew out a mouthful of air. "Calm down, Devon," she said. "People do it all the time."

Devon threw his hands up in frustration. "What is it with you Californians?" he demanded. "Group biking and wilderness trips and all kinds of West Coast craziness." His hands dropped back on the table and his shoulders drooped, all the fight gone out of him. "Maybe it's me," he said more to himself than Enid. "My life is under some black cloud. I really just don't belong anywhere."

He looked up in time to see Enid staring at him like he had two heads. It made him feel more on the outside than ever. *Maybe I should just blow out of town like I planned to,* he thought.

He pushed his plate aside and stood up. "I'm sorry," he told Enid, "but I have to go." He pulled a fifty-dollar bill out of his wallet and threw it on the table. "Dinner's on me."

"Wait, Devon! This is too much!" Enid called after him as he stormed from the table. But Devon ignored her as he left the restaurant, climbed on his motorcycle, and took off into the night.

Chapter 7

Elizabeth stood by a mountain stream Thursday evening, collecting water in her bucket so the group could boil some acorns for dinner. She and the rest of the Project Adventure members had spent the afternoon trying to catch fish with their bare hands. Gary and Kate had done most of the fishing on Tuesday. For the first time since she'd gotten to the mountains, Elizabeth had managed to catch a fish herself.

She shuddered slightly, recalling the slimy feel of the fish's skin as she worked her hands slowly toward its head and grasped it behind the gills the way Gary had shown them. Still, she couldn't help feeling a surge of pride that she'd managed to catch one of the slippery creatures. Today she and Gary were the only ones in the group who had.

Once she had collected the water, she stopped

to watch the sun as it dropped slowly behind the mountains in a splash of pink and lavender clouds. *It's so beautiful here,* she thought. *So peaceful.* But behind the peace and calm was the niggling feeling of dread. Sure, she could fish with her bare hands and set up a camp, and she knew how to find her way by following the stars or the sun. She even knew how to hunt wild animals if necessary.

But tomorrow was the group's solo night, and she knew that as soon as her solo was over, she'd have to return to Sweet Valley and face Devon and Todd. The thought of doing that seemed more challenging than anything she'd faced so far.

Making her way back to camp in the dusky light, she found the group working around the campfire.

At the sight of her new friends joking and laughing together as they worked, Elizabeth's feelings of nervous confusion faded. No matter what happened back in Sweet Valley, this would be an experience she'd never forget, with people she would always remember. "Here's the water!" she called out cheerfully as she entered the camp.

Ginny smiled, wiping her hands on her jeans. "Great," she said. "Nothing like boiled acorns and ferns to get a camper's blood racing, hey, Liz?"

Elizabeth smiled. "I'm hungry enough to eat a bear," she replied.

Dory laughed. "As long as you don't expect *me* to help you catch him," she joked.

Elizabeth grinned and poured the water into a tin pot Gary had hung over the fire.

"We'll boil the plant food first," Gary told the group, "then fry up the fish."

"Sounds good to me," Matt said as he finished peeling an acorn.

"In the meantime," Gary added, "let's talk about our solos."

There was a general groan from the group. "Do we have to?" Margaret asked. "I kind of like the group part of this adventure."

Gary smiled. "Me too," he told her. "But to graduate Project Adventure, you'll need to spend a night in the wilderness on your own. It's part of the deal," he reminded her.

Margaret sighed. "Yeah, yeah, yeah," she said. She leaned closer to him. "I won't tell if you don't," she whispered loudly.

The group laughed, and Gary shook a finger at her. "None of that, young lady," he kidded. Then his face took on a serious look. "But we really *do* have to talk about what's going to happen tomorrow, OK? So everyone gather round and let's go over what we've learned."

The group dropped what they were doing and joined Gary in a circle around the campfire.

Once they had settled in, Gary said, "As you all know by now, tomorrow—after daybreak—Kate and I will be taking each of you to a remote spot and leaving you there to fend for yourselves."

At Gary's words Elizabeth felt a thrill of anticipation and dread in the pit of her stomach. She glanced around the group. Margaret was nervously snapping a dead twig. Dory was chewing her bottom lip. Ginny and Matt were a little more composed, but their postures seemed stiffer than usual.

"I know this is a little scary," Gary told them, watching their reactions. "But you've been taking care of yourselves for six days now—you know how to find food and how to set up a camp. You know how to *survive*. And you do have the added protection of your beepers in case of an emergency."

"That's right," Kate interjected. She was sitting next to Gary, wearing a Project Adventure sweatshirt, jeans, and hiking boots. From the sweatshirt's pocket she pulled out a sheet of paper. "We're going to review what you've learned," she said, smiling confidently at the group. "Once you realize you've learned all you need to know, you won't feel so nervous. I promise."

Kate leaned forward to read the paper by the light of the campfire. "OK, first thing. How do you set up your camp?" She glanced around the group. "Matt?"

Matt took a deep breath. His silver hair glistened in the campfire's glow. "First you find a water source," he said, glancing around the group. "To do that you watch the direction different animals travel in—if a large number are heading in the same direction, it's probably because they're headed for water. Also check for more lush greenery. Plants thrive around water."

"Very good," Kate said, giving Matt a thumbs-up. "What next? Dory?"

Dory glanced around the group. "Next you set up a shelter. It gets kind of cold here at night in the mountains, if you haven't noticed," she added. The group laughed. "So you want to make a lean-to out of pine branches with the pine needles still on them to break the wind and offer some protection against rain."

"Great," Kate said. "And how do you do that, Ginny?"

Ginny took a deep breath and let it out. "You place the leaning side of the branches in the path of the wind to keep the wind from hitting you," she told the group, her forehead wrinkled in concentration. "And you should build your campfire in front of the sheltered side of the lean-to to protect the fire. If you place a small wall of rocks on the opposite side of the campfire, they'll deflect the heat into the lean-to."

"Excellent!" Kate exclaimed. "But how do you build a fire without matches?" she asked, glancing around the group. Her eyes landed on Margaret.

Margaret grinned. "I know this one cold," she said, and everyone laughed. Margaret had had more trouble than anyone trying to make a campfire. "If you have a lens of some kind, like a flashlight lens or a camera, you can focus sunlight on a pile of dry tinder. Since we don't have any kind of lenses, we need to make our campfires with wood friction."

Kate clapped, and the rest of the group joined in. "You *do* know it cold," Kate joked. She looked at Elizabeth. "Now, Liz, how do we use wood friction to make a campfire?"

Elizabeth pushed a strand of hair from her eyes. "You find some dry wood without any resin on it," she explained, recalling her first failed attempt at making a fire with some gummy pine twigs that had stuck together like glue. "Then you rub the sticks together over a pile of tinder made from dry grass and leaves. When a spark catches, you blow on it until you have a good fire started. Once that's done, you add more wood to keep the fire going."

"Wonderful!" Kate enthused. She smiled at the group. "You guys are ready. You're going to do just fine."

"I just hope I don't run into any mountain lions," Margaret joked nervously.

"Or skunks!" Ginny added with a shudder.

"You'll both do great," Elizabeth told them. "We all will." And she realized she truly meant it. Kate and Gary had taught them well, and she felt strong. *I can do this,* she told herself. And the fact was, she *had* to do this. She needed to prove to herself that she could handle life on her own.

❖　　❖　　❖

"I've had enough," Jessica said angrily as she, Lila, Amy, and Maria went careening down the road in Lila's lime green Triumph. "The Secca Lake barbecue is two days away, and the guys are showing absolutely *no* interest." Jessica stared at the passing scenery, fuming with disappointment. "I might as well have decided to throw a girls-only slumber party," she added disgustedly. "What is it with these guys anyway? The whole bunch of them are acting totally weird."

Lila downshifted to third gear as they approached a sharp curve. "That's the understatement of the year," she said, shifting back to fourth once they'd cleared the turn. She was wearing an orange T-shirt, brown slacks, and a pair of handmade kidskin racing gloves. "I haven't been able to find a single one of them after school this entire week!"

"Tell me about it," Maria complained, crossing her arms over her chest. "My so-called boyfriend hasn't called me once."

"Mine either," Amy whined. "Barry's just disappeared!"

"*I'll* show them disappeared," Jessica shot back as the group headed for the beach. "Once I get my hands on them, I'll—"

"You mean *if* you get your hands on them," Lila interrupted. "So far we've been to Guido's Pizza, the Dairi Burger, and Casey's. They're not at Todd's, shooting hoops, and they're not swimming in Bruce's pool or playing tennis on his courts." She ran a finger through her hair, steering with the opposite hand. "If you ask me, I don't even think they're *in* Sweet Valley."

"Maybe they've been abducted by aliens!" Amy exclaimed.

"If Winston comes up with *that* excuse," Maria said wryly, "he'd better be able to show me marks from the intergallactic tests they performed on him to prove it."

The girls laughed.

"I doubt even aliens could get through *those* guys' thick skulls," Jessica joked.

Lila pulled up to the beach parking lot and screeched to a stop on the sand-strewn blacktop. The four girls piled out of her sports car.

"If they're not here, I give up," Amy declared, pulling off her sandals as the group made their way over a sand dune.

Once over the dune they had a clear view of the shoreline for miles. There were a couple of kids playing in the surf, their mother watching them from a blanket on the sand. An elderly man, dressed in hip-high rubber boots and a T-shirt, was fishing, and farther down, a couple of kids about fourteen or so were holding hands and watching the waves. Other than that the beach was empty.

Lila shook her head in disgust. "Looks like they're not here either," she said. She crossed her arms and turned toward Jessica. "What do you suggest now?"

she asked. "We're pretty much out of options."

Jessica squinted at the waves, thinking. "They're up to something, that's for sure," she said, half to herself and half to her friends.

"No kidding," Lila retorted sarcastically.

Jessica shot her a withering look. "It looks like we're going to have to work a little harder at finding out what's going on with these guys. This calls for some serious detective work."

She swung around in the sand, heading back to Lila's car. "Come on, gang," she said, waving her friends on. "It's time we found out where all the guys have gone."

"Tell me more about this Trek bike," Todd said to the salesclerk at Cycle-Rama on Thursday evening.

"The Trek? She's a beauty," the salesclerk replied enthusiastically. "She's got superior tires and twenty-one speeds to help you up and down the steepest mountain," he continued, pointing them out. "And the body is lightweight but incredibly strong." He ran a hand over the panther black frame and patted the handlebars lovingly. "I'm saving to buy one of these little beauties myself."

Todd glanced sideways at the clerk. He didn't look like a biker. Beneath his sports jacket and baggy trousers he appeared to be a bag of bones. *Then again,* Todd thought, glancing at Keith, *I was surprised to learn that Keith biked too.*

"What do you think?" Todd asked, turning to Keith. Since Keith had more experience with mountain biking, Todd had asked him to come along to help him pick out the right bike. The bike he'd borrowed from Keith wasn't bad, but for the Great Mountain trek he wanted the best. He needed to psych himself up for the big ride.

Keith studied the bike, nodding in appreciation. "Top of the line, man," he said, stroking the handlebars. "It's gonna be like riding on air."

Todd threw his right leg over the seat and climbed on to get a feel for the equipment. "Nice," he said.

The salesclerk nodded seriously. "You're not gonna find any better," he stated matter-of-factly.

"I'll take it," Todd said, handing the clerk his credit card.

"Good choice," the clerk told him as he headed for the cash register.

Once the sale was rung up, Todd and Keith left the store and wheeled the bike to the parking lot, where Keith's car was waiting.

"It's a great piece of equipment," Keith said. "You're going to really notice the difference after riding that junker of mine."

Todd smiled. "Your bike wasn't so bad, Keith. Although the brakes could use some work," he said. "A couple of times going downhill I thought I was going to go straight past the mountains and into the ocean."

Keith laughed. "We would have saved you, buddy," he said. "After all, that's *my* spare bike!"

Todd grinned and punched Keith's shoulder, then climbed on his bike. "I'm gonna take my new wheels for a test drive," he said.

Keith winked. "Later, man," he said, climbing into his car.

Todd flashed Keith the peace sign, then took off. *Yeah,* Todd thought as he pulled onto the road, the bike sailing beneath him, *this is definitely a fine piece of equipment.* And it was definitely going to help him get to a better place, he decided, with or without Elizabeth.

As he pushed the bike to full speed he told himself that if Elizabeth could stand to be without him, then he could stand to be without her too. The wind blew in his face and his legs pumped harder, forcing Elizabeth out of his mind.

Chapter 8

A loud clanging startled Elizabeth awake on Friday morning. Groaning, she groggily opened her eyes to the pale pink rays of sun peeking over the horizon. "Ten more minutes," she mumbled, covering her head with her air pillow.

The clanging grew louder. "Up, up, *up!*" Gary shouted over the racket. Elizabeth moaned and reached for the zipper of her sleeping bag. "Is it time to go home yet?" she asked, forcing herself to a sitting position.

Dory laughed. "Almost, kiddo," she said as she rolled up her sleeping bag a few feet away.

"Almost, my foot," Margaret grumbled, smoothing her disheveled hair as she kicked her way out of her covers. She shook her head. "I must be crazy to have come on this trip."

Elizabeth caught Dory's eye and smiled. Of all

the members in their Outdoor Bond group, Margaret had turned out to be the crankiest in the morning. Matt, on the other hand, was already at the fire, perking coffee. *I bet he was up before Gary,* Elizabeth thought, making her way to the fire for a cup of caffeine and some of the fish that Matt was frying up for breakfast.

Kate joined her on the log that had become their living-room couch for the week. "How's it going?" she asked, taking a sip of her coffee.

Elizabeth yawned. "Pretty good, I guess. I'll know better once I'm awake."

Kate smiled. "I like early morning in the woods," she said. "There's something almost sacred about it, don't you think?"

Elizabeth took a deep breath of the cool morning air as she listened to the birds singing to the waking sun. "There is," she agreed. "It makes you feel like you're part of nature, not separate from it." She put down her tin cup and plate, searching for words. "It's like I've begun to feel my spirit in everything."

Kate nodded. "That's what I like to hear," she said. "It tells me you're ready. Once you recognize nature as something that's *part* of you instead of something you have to *conquer,* it means your instincts are in tune with your surroundings. That will help you to survive."

Elizabeth gazed at the sunrise. "I hope so," she said. *And maybe those same instincts will help me reach a decision about Devon and Todd,* she thought desperately.

The sound of a motor coming up the narrow mountain road interrupted her thoughts.

"Van's here!" Gary shouted as the group turned toward the noise.

Suddenly the area was alive with campers rolling up sleeping bags and gathering their belongings. Elizabeth forgot about Todd and Devon for the moment as she raced around the camp with the others, ticking off a mental checklist of what she needed to take. *Compass,* she told herself, *pocketknife, sleeping bag, clothes . . . beeper, don't forget the beeper!*

She hurriedly clipped the beeper to her belt and had just managed to finish zipping her duffel bag when Gary clapped and called, "OK, everyone! Time to move out!"

Elizabeth followed Ginny into the van. "This is it," Ginny said, gripping Elizabeth's hand.

Elizabeth squeezed back. "Good luck," she said as the van started up and headed farther into the mountains.

Matt was dropped off first and then Dory. Ginny and Margaret were next. *How far are they taking* me? Elizabeth wondered, glancing at Kate and Gary as the van climbed higher. Finally the driver stopped. All Elizabeth could see were trees.

"We're here," Gary said, getting out to throw open the van door for Elizabeth.

Elizabeth gulped the lump in her throat, glancing nervously at Kate.

"Don't forget what we talked about last night," Kate reminded her. "You know all you need to know."

Elizabeth nodded, feeling a little less nervous. Kate was right. She could do this.

She climbed out of the van, and Gary handed her her duffel bag. "Just remember all you've learned and you'll be fine," he told her. "If you get into real trouble, use your beeper."

"Right," Elizabeth said. "Thanks, guys," she called out as Gary climbed back into the van.

She watched them drive off, the sound of the van's engine fading in the distance until there was nothing left but the wind rustling through the trees. Picking up her duffel bag, Elizabeth breathed in the heady scent of pine, listening to the birds calling to one another from the high branches. She felt good. It was a lovely, breezy day, and the sky was a cloudless blue.

She walked through the woods until she came to a clearing. Surrounded by lush green trees and lovely rolling hills, she knew that now, at last, she had some real time to herself to think about the situation with the guys. Even though she was enjoying learning to stand on her own, Elizabeth knew that she loved Devon and Todd. And she knew it would be impossible for her to stay away from both of them. But she had to make a choice.

She couldn't continue to lead both of them on.

For a moment she pictured each guy in her mind—Todd, so loving and gentle, always there for her. Devon, who made her heart race with his sensitive brilliance, his soulful gaze.

She shook herself out of her thoughts—she didn't have time to think about that now. She had to set up camp. Then she could relax and concentrate.

Pulling out her compass to get her bearings, she laid down her gear. *If there's some water around here*, she decided, *those trees near the clearing will be a good place to set up camp.*

Noticing a flock of birds heading east overhead, she started in that direction, keeping an eye out for animal tracks headed the same way. She spotted some skunk and rabbit tracks and, a little farther along, a raccoon trail. *Looking good,* she thought, checking out some nibbled acorns under a nearby tree.

She found water not far from the clearing, a clean, ice-cold mountain stream. A doe and fawn sniffed the air as she drew closer, then bounded off into the woods. Elizabeth smiled. Kneeling beside the stream, she cupped her hands to taste the water. It was sweet and fresh. *Perfect,* she thought.

Once she'd determined that the water was OK, she checked the surrounding area for bear tracks or claw marks on the trees. Then she began to identify the various plants and trees in the area, noting a sugar pine, an oak, and a beechnut tree right off the bat. Checking out the flora, she decided she could have a dinner of pine seeds, arrowhead root, and dandelions.

As the sun rose higher in the sky she took off her sweatshirt and tied it around her waist. She felt strong and confident that she had everything under control as she trekked back to the clearing where she'd laid her gear.

Once she reached the clearing, she carried her equipment toward a clump of trees and began to gather leaf-covered branches to make her lean-to. As soon as she was finished she would build a fire. *Then I'll make my decision about Todd and Devon,* she told herself, picking up a branch and piling it near a tree.

"Check it out," Lila said, nudging Jessica as they carried their trays from the cafeteria food line Friday afternoon.

Jessica glanced at a table near the back of the cafeteria where Bruce, Todd, Aaron, and Barry were sitting, talking excitedly.

"What do you suppose they're talking about?" Maria asked, coming up behind Jessica and Lila with Amy in tow. She gave the other girls a sidelong glance as they made their way through the bustling crowd of students.

Jessica raised an eyebrow. "Only one way to find out," she said, pushing her way past a giggling group of freshmen girls and heading toward the rear of the cafeteria.

As soon as the four girls drew near the table Jessica noticed Bruce nudge Barry, who in turn nudged Todd. By the time the girls reached the table, the guys' conversation had come to a standstill.

"Don't stop on account of us," Jessica said wryly, scooting in beside Todd.

The guys laughed nervously. "We were just talking guy stuff," Barry explained weakly.

"Yeah, sports and swimsuit issues," Aaron added, making room for Lila.

"So," Todd said. "What's new?"

Jessica exchanged a glance with her friends. *The guys are still acting weird,* she thought. *What gives?*

Lila plopped her food tray on the table. "I'll tell you what's new," she told Todd, an annoyed note in her voice. "We're sick of the way you guys have been ignoring us—disappearing into thin air, avoiding us like the plague. Just what are you hiding anyway?"

"Hiding?" Aaron asked innocently, glancing at the other guys. He forced a laugh. "We're not hiding anything."

"Of course not," Bruce backed him up. "Speaking of which, has anyone seen that new movie, *Hiding from Death's Shadows?* I hear it's got these really cool special effects."

117

"Yeah?" Todd said, leaning toward Bruce, his eyes wide with exaggerated interest. "What's it about?"

"Well," Bruce began. "There are these three pilots, see, and—"

"Can it, guys," Maria interrupted him. "We don't want to hear about the latest Hollywood action flick—we want to know what's going on."

The guys glanced at one another, fidgeting nervously.

This is getting weirder and weirder, Jessica thought. She crossed her arms, studying the guys for a clue. They had obviously been excited about something before she and her friends sat down. Now they were acting like they'd been caught throwing spitballs at Principal Chrome Dome's shiny head.

"Look, guys," Jessica said, deciding to try to reason with them. "We just want to know where you've been disappearing to, that's all. What's the big deal?"

She'd barely finished the question when Todd jumped up, glancing at his watch. "Shoot! I just remembered I have to get to my biology class early to set up a lab. I gotta go," he declared, grabbing his books.

Aaron leaped from his chair. "Wait for me," he called after Todd. "I have English next, and I left my book in my locker."

Jessica's brow furrowed as Bruce and Barry

118

suddenly remembered that they were supposed to go to the office to explain being late for homeroom that morning. In a few short minutes the table was devoid of males.

Amy stared after them as the last of the guys left the cafeteria. "Can you *believe* it?" she gasped, glancing around the table incredulously.

Jessica nodded. "I told you they were up to something," she said knowingly.

"No doubt about it," Maria concurred.

"The question is, what are they hiding?" Lila wondered aloud.

The girls looked at one another, searching for an answer.

"The party will be a total bomb if none of the guys shows up," Amy said despondently.

"So what are we going to do?" Maria asked, throwing her hands up helplessly.

Jessica leaned forward in a conspiratorial way. "We're not beaten yet," she said. "We've got today and tomorrow to figure out what's going on and put a stop to it."

Lila crossed her arms and legs. "And just how do you propose to do that?" she asked skeptically.

Jessica slapped her palms on the tabletop. "I've already figured it out," she told Lila. She motioned the group to come closer. "This is the plan. We're going to follow those guys after school. We find out where they're going, and then we corner them." She sat back triumphantly.

Maria raised an eyebrow. "Follow them? How are we going to manage that without them seeing us?"

Jessica smiled confidently. "Easy," she said. "We park our cars across the street from the parking lot exit and wait until they leave school. Then we take off after them—at a distance, naturally, so they won't know they're being followed."

Lila made a dubious face. "I don't know," she said. "What if they get out of school before we do?"

"I already thought of that," Jessica informed the group, leaning closer to the table. "It's Chrome Dome's birthday next week. I talked to his secretary, Rosemary, earlier today and told her the cheerleading squad wanted to get Chrome Dome a surprise gift. I suggested it would help if we could leave a few minutes early to meet about the surprise before cheerleading practice." She smiled slyly. "Rosemary was so thrilled we were thinking of old Chrome Dome, she didn't even check to see if there really *was* a practice. She just gave me the passes."

Jessica pulled four hall passes out of her purse and fanned herself with them. "Am I good or what?" she asked, buffing her nails on her shirt.

"I have to admit, that was pretty slick," Amy said appreciatively.

"Way to go, Jess," Maria agreed.

Lila didn't seem quite so impressed. "That means we have to buy Chrome Dome a gift," she pointed out. "What on earth are we going to get

Chrome Dome for his birthday—a toupee?"

The girls laughed.

"But Lila's got a point," Amy conceded. "And how much do we have to spend?"

Jessica shook her head in disappointment. "Have you forgotten it was *me* who planned this?" she asked. Reaching into her purse again, she pulled out a plastic statue that was inscribed *World's Greatest Principal,* along with a good-sized birthday card. "We pass the card around our classes next week. Then, when it's full, we give it to Chrome Dome. He'll be so thrilled to see all the kids who remembered his birthday, it won't matter that we didn't spend a lot of money."

Lila wrinkled her nose disgustedly at the statue. "That's the cheapest birthday gift I've ever seen," she told Jessica.

Jessica lifted her chin defiantly. "I happen to be paying for a *huge* party this weekend, Lila," she said. "You're more than welcome to buy Chrome Dome something nicer if you want."

Lila rolled her eyes. "Like I want to spend my weekend hunting for a present for our principal," she retorted. She got a thoughtful look on her face. "Although maybe I'll send the chauffeur out to pick up a fruit basket. . . ."

"Whatever," Jessica interjected. "Right now we need to set our plan in motion."

Lila crossed her legs in a parody of sophistication. "Just call me Jane Bond," she quipped wryly.

The girls laughed.

"That's more like it," Jessica said, reaching into her purse again. "OK, everyone," she announced, pulling out her cell phone. "Let's check the batteries in our phones to make sure they're charged."

"I charged mine last night," Amy told her, taking a bite of her Caesar salad.

Maria pulled a cell phone from her backpack and checked the battery. "I'm good," she said.

Lila picked at her fruit salad. "Naturally my phone's fine. The chauffeur checks it every week."

"Great," Jessica said. She glanced at her wrist. "Let's synchronize our watches. According to mine, it's exactly twelve forty-six."

"Wait a minute. Since when do *you* wear a watch?" Amy asked.

"I snagged it from my mom's jewelry box this morning," Jessica said. "I had to be prepared for my plan."

Lila glanced at her watch. "Well, I have twelve forty-eight," she said, "and I *know* mine's right."

Jessica rolled her eyes. "Fine. We'll compromise. Make it twelve forty-seven," she advised the group. "We'll meet out front at two twenty-five."

"Right," Maria said, setting her watch.

Jessica smiled slyly as Amy and Lila followed suit. Operation Blow Their Cover was in motion.

Elizabeth's stomach growled for the third time in as many minutes. She'd been so wrapped up in setting up her camp, she'd forgotten that the last time she had eaten was at breakfast before being dropped off. She glanced at her watch. It was nearly five—almost twelve hours since she'd had a few bites of fish and some coffee.

Her stomach growled again. *Time to use my new survival skills to get some dinner,* she told herself. After banking the fire by adding ashes so it burned low and wouldn't go out, Elizabeth pulled her tin pail from the duffel bag and walked farther into the woods, looking for berries and roots.

The soft breeze that had been with Elizabeth in the morning had died down, leaving the woods heavy with still, hot air. Flies and mosquitoes buzzed past her ears with annoying frequency as she searched for her dinner. *I don't remember the bugs being so bad,* she thought. Of course, before today she'd always worked with the others to gather food—had someone to talk to while she worked.

But I came here to have some time on my own, she reminded herself as she slapped at a mosquito. *Insects are just part of nature.*

After walking for a good half hour and finding nothing but a few rotten acorns, she finally stumbled on a wild raspberry bush. "This is more like it," she said, relieved. She scratched herself several times on brambles before she noticed that most of the berries were green. "Now what?"

She began searching again and eventually came

across a clump of dandelions in a clearing. *Yech,* she thought, remembering their horrible bitter taste when Kate had shown the group how to boil and eat them. She glanced into her pail, where a few measly acorns, a couple of raspberries, and some beech bark sat limply at the bottom. *It's only one night,* she reminded herself. Kneeling down on a bed of moss, she began to grab handfuls of dandelions.

Sweating and tired, she stopped when the pail was halfway full. *Once this stuff is boiled down, there won't be much,* she thought, wiping a loose strand of hair from her forehead. But the bugs were getting worse, and she was famished.

She stood up, stretching to relieve her aching muscles. *A light meal is good for the soul,* she told herself. *People eat way too much anyway.*

Elizabeth carried the pail to the stream, washed off her food and added some water for boiling it, then carried it back to camp. As she waited for her dinner to cook she thought again about Todd and Devon. She had to make a decision by tomorrow morning, and she still wasn't any closer than she'd been when she got here.

She felt herself falling into a depression and stopped. *It will come to me,* she told herself. *It has to.*

It took almost an hour for the food to cook over the open fire. When it was finally done, it barely covered the bottom of the pail. Elizabeth laid down her sweatshirt as a tablecloth, dumped the contents of the pail onto her tin plate, and pulled out her folding knife and fork. She carefully cut her dinner into tiny portions and began to eat, chewing each bite thirty-two times and swallowing before taking another bite to stretch out the meal.

Once she had finished eating, she carried the plate and pail to the stream to wash them, along with her tin cup for a drink. No sooner had she finished her dishes and drunk a cupful of water than her stomach growled again.

She glanced at the sky. The sun was getting lower, the clouds thicker. There was no way she could spend another couple of hours gathering more food. *Get your mind off your stomach!* she ordered herself. *Think about something else.*

As she trudged back to camp she concentrated on thinking of something besides how hungry she was. *I wonder what Jess is doing right now,* she mused, imagining her twin all comfortable and full amidst the clutter in her bedroom. *She's probably planning that barbecue I promised I would help with. After surviving this experience, I may even be able to handle Jess's parties,* she thought, smiling wryly.

But her smile faded as her stomach growled again. If *I survive this experience,* she corrected herself.

Devon finished packing his last saddlebag and buckled it closed. He glanced around the room that had been his home for such a short while. There was nothing left of him in it. Tomorrow he would be less than a memory, a fading echo in Sweet Valley.

He sat down on the bed, running a hand through his hair. *On the road again,* he thought with grim resignation. He didn't know where he was going, just that he had to get out of Sweet Valley.

Devon fingered the handmade afghan at the foot of the bed, knowing Nan had labored over it to make him feel at home. Poor Nan. He hadn't had the heart to tell her he was leaving. It would be easier if she found out after he was gone. No crying scenes, no trying to make him stay.

He patted the afghan sadly. He really was going to miss Nan. She was the only person who had ever genuinely cared for him. His whole life he had wanted what he thought he'd found in Sweet Valley. But he hadn't counted on having his heart broken. Or on feeling so different from everyone here.

For a few crazy moments he'd actually thought that maybe, for the first time in his life, he could become part of something. Part of a community. Of a family. Of a couple . . . but it hadn't happened.

He pushed the afghan aside and his shoulders slumped. Maybe happiness wasn't part of the game plan for him, he decided. Maybe he was meant to search and search and never find what he was looking for.

Devon picked up his saddlebags, turning to look at the room one last time before he closed the door behind him. Tomorrow, from wherever he landed, he'd write Nan a letter—tell her things just hadn't worked out. Right now he had to get out of here—just leave. There was nothing left to keep him in Sweet Valley.

Chapter 9

Shortly before school got out, Jessica met Lila, Amy, and Maria on the front lawn.

"Here's the game plan," she told the other girls. "We wait across the street until we see the guys leaving, then each of us starts to follow one of their cars. Just follow whoever you can. Now let's go."

The girls hurried to their cars. Jessica grimaced as she hopped into her mother's totally uncool station wagon. The Jeep's brakes had been acting up, and the mechanic had told her not to drive it until he could check out the brakes next week. In a couple of minutes she and all her friends were parked across the street from the high school, waiting for the guys to leave.

Shortly after two-thirty Bruce peeled out of the parking lot, and Lila immediately took off after him. A moment later Jessica's mood changed when

Todd and Winston pulled out in Todd's BMW and Amy followed.

Jessica waited anxiously at the wheel of the station wagon with Maria by her side. Where were the rest of them? She looked up just in time to see Aaron and Barry pulling out of the parking lot. As they turned onto the road she noticed a couple of bikes on the rack attached to the rear of Aaron's car.

"Bikes?" Maria questioned. "What's that about?"

Jessica started the station wagon. "We're gonna find out," she said, zooming after them.

Aaron and Barry had gone about a block when they came to a traffic light.

"Jess. You're too close," Maria said anxiously as Aaron glanced in his rearview mirror.

"Duck!" Jessica ordered. She and Maria both slid down on their seats. For a moment Jessica was happy that she didn't have the Jeep. She hung back once the light changed, letting a Miata cut in between her and the guys.

"Let's go," Maria said, sitting up again. Jessica hit the gas.

Aaron and Barry drove to the outskirts of Sweet Valley, then pulled onto Mountain Road, heading east. Jessica reached for her cell phone and called Lila. "How's it going, J.B.?" she asked when Lila—alias Jane Bond—answered the phone. Jessica had thought it would be a good idea to give everyone code names in case Bruce was listening over the airwaves with the latest technodevice for intercepting phone calls. The Patmans had money to burn, and Bruce liked to blow a lot of it on all the latest gadgets.

"Bruce—uh, I mean, The Snake—last seen headed east on Mountain Road," Lila's voice came over the phone. "Not only that, but he's got a couple of bikes on the back of his car."

"Yeah?" Jessica said thoughtfully. "I noticed that Squirrel and Weasel have them too. And they're following Snake's route. I'll have Agent M. call Sherlock to see if this is the overall pattern."

"Roger," Lila said.

Maria hit Amy's speed dial number and put her on the speaker phone. "Hey, Sherlock," Jessica said. "Agent J. here with Agent M., hot on Squirrel and Weasel's trail."

"Why do we have to call Barry Weasel?" Amy complained.

Jessica groaned. "Jeez, Amy, you're not supposed to say his real name. What if Bruce is listening?"

"Good job, Agent J.," Maria said. "You just blew Sherlock *and* Snake's cover."

Jessica slapped her forehead. "Shoot! I told you we needed more rehearsal time," she declared. "Oops! Sharp curve ahead."

Jessica put down her phone and gripped the wheel of the station wagon with both hands as Aaron and Barry disappeared around a snaking curve. Maria braced herself against the car door and stared daggers at Jessica. One wrong turn and the wagon would go crashing down the side of the cliff into the ocean.

"This little mission isn't worth dying over," Maria muttered, staring ahead.

"Are you guys OK?" Amy's voice came through the speaker phone.

"Fine," Jessica said. Once she was on the straightaway again, she picked up the phone. "Where are you two?" she asked Amy and Lila.

"I just followed The Snake around a nasty curve a few minutes ago," Lila said. "It sounds like the one you just passed. I must be a few miles ahead of you, going east on Mountain Road."

"Ditto," Amy added.

"Roger. Sounds like we're hot on the same trail," Jessica said. "Over and out."

Jessica turned off her phone and continued following Aaron and Barry until they turned right into the Great Mountain National Reserve parking lot.

"Hey! Isn't this the same place Liz is bonding with Mother Nature?" Maria asked.

"Yeah. I wonder if this is a coincidence," Jessica said as she pulled off to the side of the road to phone Lila.

She hit Lila's speed dial number. "Where are you now?" she asked when Lila answered.

"Sherlock and I are stopped on the shoulder about three hundred feet from the turn into the Great Mountain Reserve parking lot," Lila told

Jessica. "We had to drive past the lot. Otherwise the guys would have seen us."

"My thoughts exactly," Jessica told her. "Do you realize that this is the same place Liz came to play cavewoman?"

"That's right!" Lila said. "You don't think Todd's here looking for Liz, do you?"

Jessica shook her head. "With five other guys?" she pointed out. "I doubt it. But it is a strange co-incidence," she said thoughtfully as she checked for oncoming traffic before pulling out into the road. "Look, stay where you are," she told Lila once she was on the road again. "Agent M. and I will meet you in a few minutes. We'll figure out our next move when I get there."

After Devon left Nan's, he hit the road, not sure where he was going or what he was going to do. He just needed to be on the move, as if the feel of the blacktop beneath him could numb his soul. *Does anything good lie ahead?* he wondered as he turned onto a winding country road. And if it did, where would he find it? He'd already driven across the country only to run into more hurt, more dis-appointment.

He drove aimlessly for what seemed like hours, lost in thought—past the beach and the lookout where he'd first seen Sweet Valley, up to Jackson's Bluff and onto another winding road.

As he drove toward the entrance of the Great

Mountain National Reserve his attention was drawn to a group of guys hanging in the parking lot. They seemed to be having a great time, slapping one another on the back, laughing and joking as they pulled mountain bikes off their car racks. For some reason a number of them looked familiar. He slowed his motorcycle to get a better look. That's when he realized it was Todd Wilkins and a group of his friends from Sweet Valley High, along with a few hippie-type guys he hadn't seen before.

Devon stopped his bike before the group noticed him and watched from a distance. It was like staring at some alien beings and their strange rituals—the high fives, the jokes, the playful punches. *Weird,* he thought. But at the same time he was drawn to the scene, fascinated by the closeness, the camaraderie of the group. *What's it like to be part of something like that?* he wondered.

Once the bikes were off the cars, Todd and his group started walking them toward the mountains. Devon hesitated a moment, but he was really curious to see what they were up to. He was, after all, a scientific genius, wasn't he? *And scientists draw conclusions from observation,* he reminded himself.

He climbed off his motorcycle and began to follow them. *Just to observe,* he told himself. Not because he longed to be part of something like this, but because he was gathering impartial information on the peculiar habits of the California male.

Sure, that was it. Just checking out the wildlife of California before he moved on. At least that's what he tried to tell himself. But deep down he knew he had nothing else to do. No place else to go. As of today, his future was a severe blank before him.

Elizabeth stood on the bank of the stream, trying to spot a fish. She'd tried to take her mind off her stomach by concentrating on making a decision about Todd and Devon, but she had begun to feel light-headed—dizzy with indecision and hunger. As much as she hated to have to search for more food, she didn't think she could make it until morning without something else to eat. She had considered gathering more dandelion greens and acorns, but it was so much work for so little food. And she felt like she hadn't eaten in days. A fish might fill her enough to get her through the night.

A ripple in the stream caught her eye. She squinted, trying to get a better look. *Yes!* she thought with a rush of relief as a fish came into focus. Pulling off her hiking boots and socks and rolling up her jeans, she waded quietly into the water so she wouldn't scare her dinner, creeping slowly toward the wriggling creature until she was close enough to grab it. She lowered her hands into the cold stream and slowly moved them toward the creature's backside.

She had barely gotten her fingers around the fish's tail when it bolted, slipping out of her grasp like jet-powered Jell-O. "Oh, great," she said, shaking the water from her hands with a frustrated sigh.

She took a deep breath. Gary had told them that in order to survive in the wilderness, they couldn't stop trying. She closed her eyes and counted to ten, then opened them again, searching for another fish. After a moment or two she caught sight of one in a shallow spot among some rocks across the stream.

Elizabeth resisted the urge to chase it as she crept across the water. *This one looks like an easy catch,* she thought, noticing how it seemed trapped among the rocks. When she was right above it, she reached down in a quick motion and yanked her hands up. Water dribbled through her fingers. She glanced down at the stream. The fish was nowhere to be seen.

Frustrated to the point of tears, Elizabeth glanced toward the underbrush near the far bank. A rabbit was crouched near some bushes, sniffing the air. She remembered what Gary had told them about trapping and killing small animals. But even with her stomach growling like an angry dog, the thought of hunting a rabbit made her nose wrinkle with disgust. There was no way she was going to hurt a cute little fur ball like that. She'd rather starve.

As the rabbit hopped away she glanced toward the horizon. It was almost sunset. Maybe she'd try to catch a fish one last time before nightfall.

Her gaze fell from the sky to the stream, past the bushes where the rabbit had been a moment before, and her heart jumped. There were two shiny, beady eyes staring at her from the underbrush! Her arms broke out in goose bumps. Was it some dangerous creature about to make her *its* dinner?

She backed out of the stream, keeping her gaze on the glowing eyes. How many hours had it been since her solo began anyway? she wondered. How many more before the arrival of her pickup at daybreak to take her back to civilization?

She climbed out of the stream and hurriedly pulled on her socks and boots. *Where are Devon and Todd when I really need them?* she asked herself as she backed toward the camp. But no sooner had the question popped into her head than she cringed. *Why should Todd and Devon be here?* she silently demanded. *I came out here to learn to survive, to learn to be on my own. I don't need anyone to save me.*

"No one," she murmured, but her gaze fell longingly to her emergency beeper, and her hand itched to press the button for someone to come and help her.

She shoved her hand in her pocket. No! She wasn't going to use the beeper. She didn't need to. *I can make it through the night,* she told herself. She took one last look at the stream. But it was going to be dark soon. There was no time left to catch a fish. Besides, she wanted to get as far away from whatever was in the bushes as she could.

She glanced past the stream to a hill about a hundred feet away. Maybe she'd take a walk to the top of that hill. Watch the sun setting over the forest. The sunsets were beautiful out here in the wilderness, and maybe—for a while—it would get her mind off her stomach and the night that lay ahead.

"OK, mount up," Keith called out when the group of bikers reached the foot of a steep hill. Todd moved up behind Keith and was just about to put on his helmet when he noticed someone lurking behind the group about a hundred feet away. He squinted to get a better look and realized who it was—Devon!

He hesitated an instant, recalling their fight at the Dairi Burger. The other day, when he had asked Devon to ride with them, he must have still been feeling good from his bike ride, he realized. Now he couldn't help recalling how furious he'd been at Devon for taking Elizabeth from him, how he'd wanted to hurt the guy the way he'd been hurt. He felt a surge of anger deep in his gut. For a second he wanted to hurt Devon again, and he hated the way it made him feel, sick and poisoned inside.

He glanced at the group of bikers, then back at

Devon, and made a split second decision. "Hey, Devon!" he called out before he could change his mind. "What brings you here?"

Devon seemed startled. For a moment Todd thought he might turn around and run. Then he called back, "I . . . uh . . ."

"You want to join us?" Todd asked, waving him over.

Aaron looked at Todd like he was crazy. "What are you doing, man? That guy stole Liz from you!"

Todd shrugged, strapping on his helmet. "I'm tired of being angry," he said. "Devon's here. I want him to join us."

Keith smiled knowingly. "It's fate, man," he said. "Patman's got an extra bike, and now we've got someone to ride it."

Barry grinned. "Yeah, Bruce's personal motto is why have just one of anything when you can have two, right, Bruce?" he quipped, slapping Bruce on the back.

Bruce frowned. "It's a spare in case *this* bike gets damaged," he said, patting the handlebars of his BMW mountain bike. "I'm not sure I want some weirdo riding it."

Todd gave him a hard look. "Devon's not a weirdo," he said. "He's just alone. How about a little generosity of spirit here?"

Bruce sighed. "OK, OK. But anything happens to the bike, he's paying," he said just as Devon joined them.

"Paying for what?" Devon asked suspiciously.

"Bruce was just saying what a workout mountain biking is," Todd improvised. "You'll be paying tomorrow with some sore leg muscles—but you can use Bruce's extra bike if you want to come ride with us."

Devon looked at the bike on the back of Bruce's car and then back at the group. He hesitated a second, then nodded. "Yeah, I'd like to try."

"Great," Todd said. "We'll wait here while you saddle up."

He watched as Devon jogged toward Bruce's car, feeling better about his decision already.

Devon felt the other guys' eyes on him as he pulled Bruce's bike from the back of the car. What had he gotten himself into anyway? He felt really awkward—a feeling he wasn't used to. He didn't know these guys. He didn't *want* to know these guys. But what else was he supposed to do when Wilkins spotted him? Confess to spying like some kind of criminal voyeur?

He rode Bruce's bike back to the mountain resignedly. He'd go through this, then he was outta here—he'd never have to see Todd or Sweet Valley again.

"OK, let's go!" Keith said when Devon reached the group. In a moment they had started up the mountain.

Whoa, Devon thought as his legs pumped

against gravity, *this is tough going!* If he were on his motorcycle, he'd practically be at the top of the mountain already. He glanced ahead, gauging the distance to the peak. *It seems like miles,* he thought, his muscles straining.

"You all right back there, Whitelaw?" a jeering voice called from ahead.

Devon glared at Bruce, who was glancing over his shoulder with a taunting grin on his face.

"Why, you need some help, Patman?" Devon called back, forcing his legs to pump harder. Devon hadn't liked Bruce from the day he met him. He had a sudden urge to catch up with the jerk *and* pass him.

Straining until he thought his legs would break, Devon passed Aaron and then Barry until he was right behind Bruce. "Falling back a little, aren't we, Bruce?" he called sarcastically, so intent on catching the guy that he didn't notice a squirrel running across the trail in front of his bike until it was almost too late.

Braking and swerving, Devon nearly went over the handlebars as he avoided hitting the frightened creature. He struggled to keep the bike upright, then stopped for a minute to catch his breath, letting the other bikers pass him.

"See you at the top!" Bruce called over his shoulder.

Yeah, Devon thought. But he decided not to take the bait this time. Acting like a maniac on a bike trail was obviously as dangerous as acting like a maniac on a highway.

Devon took a drink of water from the bottle Keith had supplied him, then climbed back onto his bike. He was here now. He might as well try to enjoy it, he decided, glancing at the lush woods and impressive mountains surrounding him.

Falling into a strenuous but unfrenzied rhythm, he began to think it wasn't half bad, riding on his own steam. There was something soothing about it—just him and the mountains, him against the terrain. It wasn't entirely different from the feeling he got riding down an open road on his motorcycle. In a few minutes he'd caught up with the group again.

"Good riding," Todd called out, glancing over his shoulder as Devon pulled up behind him.

Devon couldn't suppress a smile. "Thanks," he said, thinking Todd seemed pretty decent.

As the group continued higher and higher up the mountain Devon began to feel lighter—as if the sweat streaming from his pores was helping to wash away his ghosts. *Spin.* The painful disappointment of his uncle Pete faded, replaced by an acceptance that Uncle Pete was what he was. *Spin.* The anger he'd felt at his aunt and uncle in Ohio drifted toward the sky. *Spin.* His resentment of his parents softened—what happiness had they ever known themselves that they could have shared with him?

He felt a rush of sadness and relief as a couple of very unfamiliar tears worked their way to the corners of his eyes, mixing with his sweat and falling to the ground. As the sun touched the horizon he biked higher and higher up the mountain, leaving the tears far behind.

Chapter 10

The sun had turned the clouds to smudges of tangerine against a violet sky as Elizabeth climbed toward the top of the hill. She had stooped to examine an unusually pretty wildflower when she heard what sounded like some guys whooping and laughing. She shook her head, like someone coming out of a daze. *It must be the hunger,* she thought. *It's making my mind play tricks on me.* She was, after all, in the middle of nowhere. There was no one around for miles.

Straightening up, she continued on her way to the top of the hill. Reaching the summit a few minutes later, she sat on a boulder to study the sky, the streaks of magenta and orange on the horizon.

But no sooner had she sat than she heard another human-sounding cry.

Her head turned toward the sound, and she

saw Devon flying through the air. She shut her eyes tightly. *Now I know I'm imagining things,* she told herself, opening them in time to see Devon tumble and hit the ground.

This is crazy, she thought. Crazier still when she saw Todd flying after him, as if the fight at the Dairi Burger had spiraled into surreal proportions.

"OK, OK," she said aloud, trying to calm herself. "I've read about this. It's a vision, that's all. My mind is taking all the stress of the past couple of weeks and turning it into some kind of weird hallucination."

She watched—frightened but at the same time fascinated—to see how the vision would work itself out. Maybe it held the answer for her. Maybe it was her mind showing her which one of the guys to choose. She sighed. Or maybe it was just a replay of the Dairi Burger scene. Devon and Todd would start fighting, and she'd be right back to where she started from.

She stared harder, trying to make sense of what she was seeing as Todd approached Devon. *Here it comes,* she thought. *Todd's going to punch Devon, and Devon's going to hit him back.* But even as she thought it, she realized that Todd wasn't going to fight Devon. He was offering Devon his hand.

Elizabeth rubbed her eyes. Was her mind making her see what she'd been wishing for—the two guys she loved actually acting civil, like decent human beings?

As she continued watching she suddenly became aware of the helmets Todd and Devon were wearing and the bikes on the ground where Devon had fallen. *Mountain bikes?* she thought incredulously. Cool, cerebral Devon, hurling downhill on a *mountain* bike?

Suddenly there was more movement from the hill. She stared openmouthed as Bruce, Winston, Keith, and Barry sped down the hill after Devon and Todd. Her head spun like the wheels of their bikes. *What could this possibly mean?* she wondered. It was like watching some weird art movie—like living in a dream—except she knew she was awake.

She watched the group in amazement, totally freaked out by the whole vision. *It can't get any weirder than this,* she thought. At least that's what she believed until she heard the crunch of shoes on mountain rocks and turned to see Jessica coming up behind her, followed by Lila, Maria Santelli, and Amy.

"Lizzie, omigod! What are *you* doing here?" the Jessica vision exclaimed.

Elizabeth shook her head like a dog shedding water, trying to get this crazy vision out of her brain. But the illusions were as sharp as ever. "You're not really here," she said out loud, hoping her voice would break the spell.

"What's wrong with her?" the Lila illusion asked the Jessica vision. "And why are we climbing *this*

147

hill—the guys are on *that* one," she said, pointing to the group of guys.

Elizabeth groaned. It was getting worse. She put her hand on her emergency beeper. She must really be ill. Feverish. Deluded.

The Jessica vision crossed her arms over her chest. "Do you know those bozos have been out here playing in the dirt *all week* instead of helping us plan the party?" it asked Elizabeth angrily.

Elizabeth stared at the Jessica vision. That sounded *exactly* like something Jessica would say. Elizabeth could even smell the delicate jasmine perfume Jessica wore. "You sure don't smell like an illusion," she muttered.

The Jessica illusion reached out and pinched Elizabeth's arm.

"Ow!" Elizabeth cried, rubbing the sore spot. "That didn't *feel* like an illusion either."

Jessica blew out an exasperated breath. "That's because it's *not* an illusion, Liz," she said. "None of this is," she added, opening her arms to incorporate Lila, Maria, Amy, and the whole Great National Reserve. "We're really here." She glanced down. "Just look at the mess this mud has made of my cute boots," she added despondently.

Elizabeth stood up. Only Jessica would worry about getting a pair of hiking boots muddy. "You *are* real, aren't you?" she asked incredulously, touching Jessica's arm.

Jessica rolled her eyes. "You've been out here

way too long, Lizzie," she said, shaking her head. "Of course I'm real." She glanced disgustedly toward the other hill, where the guys were standing around, talking and laughing. "And those morons are actually going up and down the mountain on their bikes," she added, flinging an arm toward the guys. "Although for the life of me, I haven't got a clue why."

Elizabeth looked to where Jessica was pointing. Todd and Devon were smiling at each other—actually talking and laughing together. A smile crept across Elizabeth's face. Maybe Jessica couldn't understand it, but Elizabeth thought she did. The Todd and Devon standing on the next mountain weren't the animals she'd accused them of being. They were the two guys she had fallen in love with. They'd worked things out between themselves because that's what smart, strong guys did—reasoned things out with their brains, not their fists.

A wave of warmth and admiration spread over Elizabeth. She was so proud of the two of them, and she loved them both so much. And for this one moment in time that felt all right.

"What do you say, gang, time to crash the party?" Jessica suggested, breaking Elizabeth's spell.

"I'm game," Maria said, picking up a pine cone and tossing it into the woods. "I've had enough of the great outdoors for one day, thank you very much."

"And I've got a few bones to pick with that

Bruce," Lila added. "I nearly crashed my Triumph following him here. He drives like a maniac!"

"I still don't understand why we had to code-name Barry Weasel," Amy lamented, looking toward the group of guys. "He's more like an eagle or something, you know? Not some squirrely little animal."

Jessica shot Amy a look. "Are you going to whine about that for the rest of the weekend?" she asked impatiently. "He's an eagle, then, all right? Barry's nickname is Eagle." She straightened the collar on her denim jacket. "Now what do you say we go over there and have a talk with those guys about the party?"

Lila, Jessica, Amy, and Maria started down the hill, but Elizabeth held back. "No!" she called out before they'd gone ten feet. "Let them do their thing, or they'll probably boycott the Secca Lake party altogether."

Jessica stopped in her tracks and turned toward Elizabeth. "They wouldn't dare," she said with a scowl.

Lila looked thoughtfully at the guys and gave Jessica a doubtful look. "I wouldn't be too sure, Jess," she said. "They've been disappearing on us all week. Who's to say tomorrow night won't be the same thing?"

Maria tapped a finger against her chin. "Elizabeth and Lila have a point," she observed. "Maybe we should give the guys their space."

Elizabeth nodded. "They'll come back to us

when they're ready," she told the group. "I promise. And they'll be different—better."

Jessica gave Elizabeth a funny look. "How do you know that?"

Elizabeth smiled mysteriously. "I just do," she told her twin.

"Can we make a decision here one way or the other?" Lila asked impatiently. She plucked a leaf out of her hair and flicked it to the ground. "I hate hiking."

Jessica ignored Lila's complaining and stepped closer to Elizabeth. "You're sure about this," she said. "I mean, what if the guys don't show up at the party tomorrow night? What'll we do then?"

Elizabeth touched Jessica's shoulder. "They'll show up," she said. "I know they will."

Jessica shook her head. "But how?" she asked skeptically.

Elizabeth smiled. "Some things you just feel."

Jessica glanced undecidedly at the group of boys and then back at Elizabeth. She hesitated a moment, then said, "OK. I'm going to trust you, Liz. But you'd better be right."

"So are we going or what?" Lila demanded. "I'm famished."

"Ditto," Maria said.

"We're going," Jessica told her. "I'm hungry too. We'll sneak out the same way we came."

Jessica and her friends started down the mountain. Jessica looked back at Elizabeth when she noticed

Elizabeth hadn't moved. "Aren't you coming?" she asked. "It's time for a major chow down at Dairi Burger." She glanced around the mountains. "I don't know what you've been eating up here, but it can't be better than the Dairi Burger's bacon double cheese-burger and fries."

At the thought of tasty, warm food Elizabeth's stomach growled. She glanced at the horizon. The sky had darkened to late dusk. Soon it would be nighttime, and the air smelled like rain. She almost said yes. Yes to a good dinner with her sister and her friends, yes to a night in a warm comfortable bed.

But she'd made a pact with herself that she would see this survival week through. And she would be OK on the mountain tonight. They'd all be OK, no matter what happened. She knew that now.

She smiled at Jessica. "Thanks anyway," she said, "but I think I'll stay here."

Jessica shrugged. "Whatever. See you later, sis."

"Later," Elizabeth told her. Then she watched Jessica and her friends until they had disappeared from sight.

"You're sure you're all right?" Todd asked Devon as they picked their bikes up from where they were lying in a heap on the ground. Devon had taken a nasty fall, hitting a pothole none of the others had seen in the lengthening shadows of dusk. The rest of them had somehow miraculously ridden around it.

Devon nodded. "Yeah, just a little bruised," he told Todd. "Nothing serious."

"Nothing serious for you, maybe, but what about my bike?" Bruce demanded, checking out a dent in the handlebars.

Devon glanced sideways at Todd. "I'll buy you a new one," he said, reaching for his wallet.

At the exchange between Bruce and Devon the guys glared at Bruce, giving him a "bad move" look.

Bruce sighed resignedly. "Forget it," he said. "It's only a bike."

Todd slapped Bruce on the back. "That's more like it, Patman," he told Bruce. "Now, what do you say we head back to our cars?"

"Cool," Keith said, climbing onto his bike.

They had to pedal back up the hill before they could head down the other side. Todd went first. By the time the group reached the parking lot, Todd was panting, his pulse racing from the exertion and the thrill. "Whoo, great ride!" he yelled. "I feel like a million bucks!"

Devon pulled up beside him, breathing hard. "Listen, man," he said, looking a little sheepish. "I just wanted to say thanks for helping me out back there."

Todd shrugged. "No problem," he said. "You would have done the same for me."

Devon looked a little surprised at that, then thoughtful. "Yeah, I think I would have," he said. "But I wanted to say thanks for asking me to join the group too. It's helped me get some things straight in my head that have been bothering me for a long time," he explained. He looked thoughtfully at the last weak rays of sun sinking behind the horizon. "You know, we've all got baggage we need to get rid of now and then. I've been carrying mine around for a long time. Thanks for helping me unload it." He offered Todd his hand.

Todd shook Devon's hand, doing his best to hide the surprise he felt at Devon's gratitude. That had been a heavy thing for Devon to tell him, he realized. There must be things in Devon's past that had been pretty rough on him. Who was Todd to judge whether he was a jerk or a good guy? Maybe Devon wasn't so bad after all, even if he *did* try to steal Elizabeth. Of course, it wasn't like he could *help* falling in love with her.

"The biking helped me a lot too," Todd confessed. "I was pretty angry about what happened between you and Liz, but I guess neither of you did it on purpose." He stared at the ground. "Sometimes things happen that you don't have any control over. I guess I just didn't like the idea of not being able to do anything about it."

Devon nodded. "Yeah," he said. "I've been trying to work out my past for so long, I kind of lost sight of the fact that I'm living right *now*—that my past is something I can't change." He smiled slightly. "The ride helped me see that."

Todd pulled off his helmet. "I know what you mean," he said. "I didn't think I could stand being without Liz. But now, as much as I still want to be with her, I know I'll be all right."

"Yeah," Devon agreed. "I feel the same way."

They stood silently beneath the darkening sky for a moment. "You know what I think?" Devon said, breaking the silence. "I think if Liz wants to be alone, we should let her be. She obviously needs some space to deal with her emotions, and I, for one, haven't been giving her that space."

Todd scratched his head. "I suppose I haven't either," he admitted.

Devon glanced toward the mountain as the rest of the guys sailed into the parking lot. "What do you say we both stay away from Liz for a while?" he suggested. "Let her make up her own mind about who she wants to be with?"

Todd nodded. "Agreed," he said, sticking out his hand.

As Todd and Devon finalized their vow Aaron rode past them. "Man, what a high!" he said, throwing his hands in the air. "I could eat a horse."

Devon and Todd looked at each other and grinned.

"Anybody for Guido's?" Todd suggested.

The mountains echoed with a resounding, *"Yes!"*

Chapter 11

Elizabeth dreamed she was lying on soft moss near a warm campfire, covered by a featherweight blanket of rabbit's fur. She snuggled deeper into the moss and pulled the fur blanket closer, sighing with contentment.

"Liz, wake up," a voice broke into her dreams.

She frowned in her sleep. "Ten more minutes," she muttered, burying her head deeper in the rabbit's fur.

Suddenly she was being shaken. *Earthquake*, she thought groggily.

"Come on, Liz," Jessica's voice said loudly in her ear. "I know you were up all night in the woods, but it's three o'clock in the afternoon. Time to get up."

Elizabeth turned over in her warm, comfortable bed. "Just a little longer, please," she murmured.

"Lizzie, now!" Jessica commanded. "You said you'd help with the party preparations, and the party's a few hours away!"

Elizabeth groaned and opened her eyes, squinting at the strong afternoon sun sifting through the shades. "OK, OK," she mumbled. "I'm up."

"Good," Jessica said, sitting on the edge of Elizabeth's bed as Elizabeth propped a pillow between her head and the headboard. Jessica glanced at the clock on Elizabeth's bed stand. "It's a little past three," she said. "Lila's picking me up in a few minutes to get the picnic area ready for the party. All you have to do is get the party trays from the deli and bring them to the lake." She glanced at Elizabeth's tousled hair and wrinkled nightshirt. "Naturally you'll need to get showered and dressed too."

Elizabeth pushed a strand of hair out of her eyes. Jessica was already dressed for the party, wearing a glittering pale blue top that brought out the color of her eyes and a black miniskirt. Her nails were painted pale blue to go with the top.

"Nice outfit," Elizabeth observed.

Jessica got up and spun around. "Isn't it?" she said, smiling. "I got it on sale at Lisette's."

"I don't know what I'm going to wear," Elizabeth told her, frowning as she climbed out of bed and went to her closet. Unlike Jessica, she didn't keep an assortment of party outfits. Everything in her closet looked like school. "It's hopeless."

158

"Maybe not," Jessica said with a twinkle in her eye. Then she went running to her room.

What's she up to? Elizabeth wondered as the sound of shoes, boxes, and coat hangers being thrown around Jessica's already messy room drifted across the hallway. A moment later Jessica came running back with a box from Lisette's and a pair of open-toed white mules with a short chunky heel. "I figured you wouldn't have time to go looking for a party outfit," she said, "so I bought you these."

Elizabeth looked from the box to Jessica and back to the box again, totally taken aback. "You got me something to *wear?*" she asked, half thrilled that Jessica had thought of her when she was shopping and half anxious at the thought of the outrageous outfit Jessica might have purchased. "That was really nice of you," she said.

Jessica waved away the thanks. "Can't have my favorite twin sister looking like a frump at my party, now, can I?"

Elizabeth smiled, then looked at the box Jessica had handed her. *Oh, well,* she thought. *How bad can it be?*

She opened the box to a pleasant surprise. Jessica had bought her a long, straight purple skirt made of cutout velour with a lavender silk lining showing through the cutouts, a sexy slit up the side, and a lavender silk blouse. Stylish but not outrageous. "It's beautiful!" she said with genuine delight.

159

Jessica grinned. "I tried to pick out something you'd like but with *my* sense of style," she said jokingly.

Elizabeth smiled at her twin, realizing how glad she was to be home. It had been great learning the things she'd learned with Project Adventure—conquering the solo on her own, making friends with such an inspiring group of people. But this was where she belonged. Besides, dealing with Jessica was an everyday challenge—with just as many rewards.

Elizabeth gave Jessica a big hug. "Thanks for the beautiful outfit," she said, squeezing her sister tightly. "Promise me we won't fight anymore."

Jessica squeezed her back. "Never again," she told Elizabeth solemnly.

Todd splashed on the cologne that Elizabeth had given him last Christmas and pulled on a blue-and-white-striped shirt. It was a few hours before Jessica's party, and he had to see Elizabeth. He needed to tell her how sorry he was, how he'd been so afraid of losing her, he'd actually ended up pushing her away.

As he combed his hair he thought about the promise he'd made to Devon that he would stay away from Elizabeth. He felt a twinge of guilt but pushed it aside. He intended to give Elizabeth her space, just like he'd promised Devon. But he needed to let her know that he still cared, that he'd be waiting if and when she decided she wanted to see him again.

He had considered calling Elizabeth, but that seemed too impersonal. Some things needed to be talked about in person. And what he hadn't explained to Devon—what he hadn't even been thinking about when he'd made the vow to stay away from Elizabeth—was that he and Elizabeth had a long history together. They'd known each other since the second grade, had gone through good times and bad together. To just stop seeing her without any explanation, without any closure to the events that had broken them apart, was something he couldn't live with. He knew in his heart that Elizabeth must feel the same way.

Once he finished dressing, Todd grabbed his car keys from the bureau and headed downstairs. A crystal vase filled with fresh-cut spring flowers was sitting on the lowboy in the hallway. The delicate scent of orchids filled the air.

Todd studied the flowers a moment, resisting the urge to pluck out a purple orchid and bring it to Elizabeth. He didn't want Elizabeth to think he was trying to win back her love with presents. That he was putting any pressure on her. All he wanted to do was apologize and ask for her forgiveness.

As he gazed at the flowers he realized he'd learned a lot in the past week. And one of those lessons was that there were some things you couldn't buy—like the feel of the sun on your face, fresh air rushing through your lungs, and friendship. And he wanted Elizabeth to be his friend. Because as much as he loved her as a girlfriend, he also loved her as a person. He needed to tell her that too.

Turning away from the flowers, Todd strolled out the front door to his car. If Elizabeth was going to the Secca Lake party tonight, maybe they could go together—not as a couple but as good friends. Naturally that would be up to Elizabeth.

He felt good as he climbed into his car and headed toward Elizabeth's house. Whatever happened, he thought, he'd be all right.

"I was so worried you were gone for good," Nan told Devon as they sat on her back porch swing, enjoying a cool breeze. "I came home and looked in your room. It seemed so empty. . . ."

Devon reached over and patted Nan's hand. When he'd come home last night from the Great Mountain Reserve, Nan had been sitting by herself in the living room, her eyes rimmed with red.

"I'm sorry, Nan," Devon said, squeezing her fingers. "I didn't mean to make you worry last night."

No one had ever worried about him before. Deep down he had thought she might even be relieved that he was gone—might enjoy having her house to herself again.

But the relief on her face when he had returned had hit him like a fist. Poor Nan had been fretting that he was gone. That she'd never hear from him again. Except for the letter he had planned to send her from the road, she probably never would have.

"Would you like a glass of lemonade?" he asked, rising from the swing to get a glass for himself.

"That would be nice," Nan told him with a contented smile.

As Devon walked to the kitchen he realized that the bike trip really had helped him to see things more clearly. Not only was he less angry at his parents and his other relatives, but his armor wasn't quite so thick anymore.

It never would have occurred to him before yesterday that Nan might miss him. Now he realized that if *he* refused to feel anything for anybody, he couldn't possibly know when they were feeling something for *him.* Feelings were like swinging doors, he surmised. They couldn't swing one way without swinging back the other. And a person couldn't shut out the bad feelings without shutting out the good.

I need to see Elizabeth, he concluded as he poured Nan's homemade lemonade into two tall, ice-filled glasses. Even though he'd suggested to Todd that neither of them should see Elizabeth for a while, the thought of her hating him was tearing Devon up inside.

Of course Devon would have liked to win her back, but that wasn't the real reason he was so desperate to see her. As much as he wanted her to love him and as much as he wanted to be with her, he needed more than anything to apologize to her. To ask her forgiveness.

The fact was, if Elizabeth didn't want to be anything more than friends, that was fine with him. Good friends were hard to come by. His whole life he'd had only one—that lady out back, sitting on the porch, happy just to have him around.

Even if Elizabeth didn't want to be friends with him, he needed to apologize for his own good, to get it out of his system. That was something else he'd learned on the bike trip—if you don't let things out, they fester inside you, turning whatever good there is to bad.

He carried the lemonade outside and drank his down in a couple of gulps. "Nan, do you mind if I go out for a while?" he asked. "There's something I have to do."

Nan nodded, a soft smile curling her lips. "I don't mind anything you do, Devon," she told him. "As long as you remember I love you."

Devon leaned over and kissed her on the forehead. "It's a deal," he said. Then he pulled out the keys to his motorcycle and headed out the door.

"How does that look?" Jessica asked Lila, stepping back to get a better view of the lanterns hung by the lake.

Lila studied the scene carefully. "I think we

need more lanterns by the dock," she said. She looked around her. "Maybe a few more over the picnic area," she added.

Jessica wrinkled her nose. "I don't know," she said. "Then it'll look like broad daylight."

"No way," Lila said, pushing a gold comb more tightly into her swept-back hair. "A soft mood doesn't mean you've got to feel your way around in the dark," she noted wryly.

"And too much light means you might as well be in the mall parking lot," Jessica argued.

"Look," Lila said, sitting down to shake a pebble from her high-heeled sandals. "You asked me my opinion, and I gave it to you. I think you need more lights, and no matter what you say, I'm not going to change my mind," she added obstinately.

Jessica sighed in exasperation. "I need a third opinion," she said, looking around for Maria or Amy. Although both girls had gotten to the lake early to help with the preparations, neither was in sight—just Bruce, Aaron, and some of the other guys who'd stopped by to help. *No use asking any of them,* she thought flatly. *They wouldn't know a lantern from a halogen lamp.* "But maybe one of them knows where I can find Amy or Maria," she said aloud, snapping her fingers.

"What?" Lila demanded.

"Nothing," Jessica said. "Do me a favor and start putting the tablecloths on, would you? I've got to get another opinion before I feel sure the atmosphere is right."

Lila shook her head in disbelief. "Oh, right. Use me like a pack mule," she said sarcastically. "I've only been to some of the best parties in some of the best homes around the world. What would *I* know about decorating an event?"

Jessica rolled her eyes. "This isn't a debutante ball, Li," she said. "I just want to make sure it's got a fun atmosphere. You know, not too formal."

Lila reached for the bag of plastic tablecloths. "I don't see why they call them cloths when they're made of this disgusting stuff," she said, pulling a covering out of the bag with the tips of two fingers.

Jessica laughed. "You won't catch a disease from them," she said as Lila cautiously spread a plastic tablecloth over one of the picnic tables.

"Synthetics and I don't agree," Lila told her.

Jessica smiled and headed for the group of guys near the lake. They'd gotten to Secca Lake early without even having to be called and had started assembling grills, hauling charcoal and coolers, and hanging lanterns around the lake without having to be prodded.

As Jessica drew nearer the group of guys, the Droids finished setting up their instruments and started to play, shaking the trees with acoustic vibrations. "Wow!" Jessica enthused, stopping next to Aaron to listen for a minute. "This party is going to be *fab*ulous!"

"What's that?" Aaron yelled, leaning closer to her so he could hear above the music.

"Fabulous!" Jessica repeated at the top of her lungs. "This party is going to be *great.*"

"You look great too!" Aaron shouted.

"Not *you*, the *party.*" Jessica laughed.

"Huh?" Aaron looked confused.

Jessica laughed again and pulled him off toward the dock, where the band was less intrusive. "What I was saying back there is that the party's going to be great," she told Aaron once the ringing in her ears had stopped.

"Oh!" Aaron said, understanding lighting his eyes. "But what I said still stands. You *do* look great."

Jessica smiled coyly. "Why, thank you, Aaron," she said, shaking back her hair. She turned toward the lake, where one of the guys had just turned on the lights to test the bulbs.

"Oooo," Jessica purred. "That looks wonderful! Lila thinks we need more lights by the lake and the dock, but I think it looks perfect just the way it is." She looked around anxiously. "If only I could talk to one of the other girls about it," she said. "You know, get another opinion."

Aaron raised an eyebrow. "Don't guys' opinions count?"

Jessica looked at him in surprise. "I guess," she told him. "I just didn't think you'd have one. I mean, I didn't know you were into decorating."

"I know what I like," Aaron told her. "And

what's nice about the night is that the light is softer than in the daytime." His brow wrinkled as he searched for words, staring at the lanterns along the lake. "You want *some* light, but I think you want it to look more like moonbeams reflected on the water—soft and diffused, not glaring."

Jessica stared at him, openmouthed. "Wow, Aaron," she said. "It sounds like you've really thought about this."

He turned his gaze from the water to her and smiled. "Nature's a pretty awesome thing," he said. "I hadn't realized how awesome until recently."

He's talking about the mountains, Jessica thought. She glanced at the lantern light rippling on the lake, thinking about how romantic it all was. *Well, if he wants to be all secretive about his mountain biking, I guess I can play along,* she decided, returning his smile. *No need to stir up the wrong kind of fire.*

Turning back toward the lake, she studied the lights on the water. "You know, what you said about the moonbeams and everything—I just thought the lanterns looked prettier that way. I never really considered why," she told Aaron, all the while thinking, *Wait till I tell Lila* this *one.* "I should be getting back to help with the tablecloths."

"Good idea," a voice from behind her said.

Jessica turned around. It was Keith Wagner.

"I asked Bruce and Winston over to help Lila when I noticed the trouble she was having getting those tables set up," Keith explained. "She looked overwhelmed."

Jessica stared at Keith in disbelief. This hippie, who seemed like he wouldn't have noticed whether his socks matched, had actually noticed that Lila needed help and had *gotten* her some! Jessica glanced over to where Lila was setting up the tables. Not only Bruce and Winston were there, but Barry as well. *What is going on?* Jessica wondered incredulously.

"I have to check the ice in the cooler," she mumbled hurriedly, rushing back to Lila to tell her what Keith and Aaron had just done. When she reached the picnic tables, Lila was simply standing there, looking totally freaked out by the guys working around her.

"Is it me, or are the guys acting way different?" Lila asked in amazement when Jessica joined her.

Jessica glanced at the tables, set up as nicely as any of the girls could have done. "I think they're different," she answered.

Lila nodded. "You know something? I kind of like it."

Jessica laughed. "Why, because they're doing your work for you?" she joked.

Lila gave her a sidelong glance. "No, because they seem more interesting somehow," she answered.

Thinking back to Aaron's romantic description of the lights on the water, Jessica had to agree. These guys definitely *were* more interesting.

Chapter 12

After Elizabeth finished putting on the new clothes Jessica had bought her, she checked herself out in the full-length mirror on the back of her bedroom door and smiled. It was a beautiful outfit, just her style. And Jessica had been so sweet to think of her. Exasperating as her twin could be, at times like these Elizabeth figured she'd love Jessica even if they *weren't* sisters.

She picked up a tube of pale pink lipstick from her bureau and had just begun to apply it when the doorbell rang. *Who could that be?* she wondered. She hurriedly blotted her lips with a tissue, then ran downstairs.

Todd was standing on the doorstep when she opened the front door. He smiled shyly. "Hi, Liz," he said.

"Todd!" Elizabeth exclaimed, totally taken aback. "What are you doing here?"

Todd glanced at his feet and back at Elizabeth. "I need to talk to you," he told her, adding hurriedly, "not about getting back together or anything like that. I just need to get things straight with you."

Elizabeth nodded. She knew how it felt to have loose ends dangling over your head. "Come in, Todd," she said. "Let's get something to drink."

Todd followed her to the kitchen. "You look beautiful tonight," he said as he settled onto a stool at the kitchen counter.

Elizabeth smiled at him. "Thanks," she said, smoothing the skirt. "Jess bought it for me."

"It brings out the blue in your eyes," Todd observed.

Elizabeth felt a blush creep to her cheeks. *Why am I feeling shy with Todd?* she wondered. Things had changed, she supposed. Even in the short time they'd been broken up, both of them had changed.

"Cola OK?" she asked, reaching into the fridge for a couple of cans of soda.

Todd nodded. "Thanks," he replied.

Once Elizabeth had gotten their drinks, she sat down on a stool across the counter from him. "So, what have you been up to?" she asked, deciding she shouldn't mention that she had seen him and Devon on the mountain last night. That was something personal between the two of them.

Todd took a drink of his soda. "Believe it or not, I've started mountain biking," he told her.

"Really?" Elizabeth said, hoping she sounded surprised.

Todd nodded. "I needed something to get my mind off what happened between us, and I started biking to forget. But then things changed. There was something about being in nature, out there with nothing but the sky and trees, that made me realize things about myself that I hadn't before. Like that you weren't just my *girl*friend, you were my friend."

"Todd, I know—," Elizabeth began.

"Before you say anything," Todd interrupted, "I just want to apologize. I'm really sorry for putting you on the spot at the Dairi Burger, and I want you to know that if you ever need me for anything— anything at all—I'm still here for you." He looked into Elizabeth's eyes.

Elizabeth met Todd's gaze, touched by his gentleness and consideration. She wanted to jump off the stool, run to his side of the counter, and give him a big bear hug—to tell him she knew that he'd grown recently.

But things had changed between them—in the short time they'd been apart, they'd each veered off onto different paths. They'd learned things about themselves they hadn't fathomed before, and Elizabeth knew that at least for her, one of those things was that she didn't need a guy to make her complete anymore.

Hugging Todd was something the old Elizabeth would have done, something the old Todd would have wanted her to do—a gesture of their mutual need for each other. Instead she put her hand on his, respecting the new boundaries between them. "I'm here for you too," she told him.

Todd opened his mouth to say something, but before he could, the phone rang. She grabbed it quickly. "Yes?" she said into the receiver.

"This is the Valley Deli," the voice on the other end said. "There are five trays of assorted meats and cheeses here, ordered by a Miss Jessica Wakefield. We close in half an hour."

Elizabeth inhaled sharply. "I'll be right there," she said.

As soon as she hung up, Elizabeth's hand flew to her mouth. Where was her *brain?* Jessica had asked her to do this one little thing, and she had completely forgotten.

"What's the matter?" Todd asked her, pushing himself off the stool as Elizabeth fumbled for the keys to the Jeep.

"That was the Valley Deli," she answered hurriedly. "Jessica asked me to pick up some trays for the party, and I forgot. The deli closes in half an hour!"

The keys dropped from her fingers as she reached for her purse. "Omigod!" she cried. "What's wrong with me?"

Todd jumped off his stool and picked up the keys for her. "Calm down, Liz," he said, touching her shoulder. "You're probably still exhausted from your Project Adventure trip."

"I *am* tired," she told him. "But I promised Jess

I'd do this for her. She's waiting for me now." She reached for the keys, but Todd clutched them in his hand.

"I'll go," he said. "You won't enjoy yourself tonight if you have to go crazy trying to get the trays to Secca Lake. I'll take a shortcut to the deli. I'm ready to go to the party anyway. It'll be easier for me to pick up the trays than it would be for you."

Elizabeth felt her panic subside. "Oh, Todd, that would be such a help," she said gratefully.

"No problem," Todd told her. Placing her keys back on the counter, he started for the door.

"Wait!" Elizabeth cried when he was halfway out of the kitchen. "Take the Jeep. Jessica's ordered five huge trays of food, and it'll be easier to fit them in the back of a Jeep than a BMW. I'll drive your car to the party and meet you there. We can talk some more," she added.

Todd smiled. "Sounds good," he said, taking the keys from her and handing her his.

"See you," Elizabeth said. It wasn't until the Jeep pulled out of the driveway that she realized she had forgotten to tell him she forgave him.

Just as Todd was pulling out of the driveway in Elizabeth's Jeep, he noticed a motorcycle turning onto her street. As it headed his way he saw by the light of a streetlamp that it was Devon.

Todd's blood boiled. *So this is the kind of*

promise Devon keeps, he thought angrily. *Playing me for a sucker so he can have Elizabeth to himself.* "Well, we'll just see about *that,*" he muttered.

As soon as Devon pulled into Elizabeth's driveway Todd jumped out of the Jeep. "What are *you* doing here?" he demanded, storming toward Devon's bike.

Devon turned off the motorcycle's engine and calmly pulled off his helmet. "Todd," he said. "What a surprise."

Todd glared at him. "Didn't we have a deal?" he demanded angrily. "Or have you forgotten already?"

Devon's jaw tightened. For an instant Todd thought Devon was going to hit him. He tightened his fists, getting ready to defend himself. But Devon took a deep breath and seemed to get himself under control.

"*I* thought the deal worked both ways," Devon retorted. "What are *you* doing here?"

It was all Todd could do to keep from rushing Devon and slamming him into his flashy bike. "Look, Whitelaw, Elizabeth and I have been friends since second grade," Todd said angrily. "We've gone through a lot together. If you think I'm giving up our friendship *that* easily, you're crazy." With that he shoved Devon, too furious to control himself any longer.

Todd waited for Devon to retaliate—throw a punch or shove him back. But Devon just stood there, glaring at him.

"I'm not going to fight you, Wilkins," Devon said.

Devon's cool, calm facade angered Todd even more. "Come on," he sneered, shoving Devon again. "You started it, now let's finish."

Devon crossed his arms and shook his head. "Yesterday you said this whole *thing* was finished," he reminded Todd. "Was that just for show around your biking buddies?"

Todd would have liked to sock Devon right then to wipe that smug look off his face. But he'd already wasted a good five minutes, and the deli was closing soon. *Liz needs me,* he thought. He didn't want to let her down.

Glaring at Devon, Todd hopped into the Jeep. "I'll see you later," he warned Devon as he peeled out of the driveway.

Before Todd turned the corner of Elizabeth's street, the last thing he saw in his rearview mirror was Devon, shaking his head.

What was that about? Devon wondered as Todd sped away. Not twenty-four hours ago the two of them had been laughing and talking together in the mountains, pouring out their hearts to each other like old friends. And now, suddenly, Todd was flying off the handle like a crazy man.

Of course, he and Todd had made a promise not to see Elizabeth, which neither of them had kept. Devon couldn't help smiling at the thought of it—both of them showing up here at the same time. It was kind of funny in a pathetic way. *That Wilkins has no sense of humor,* he decided. The fact that they'd both come to see Elizabeth tonight just showed how much they both loved her, and they'd discussed all that yesterday.

Yeah, yesterday, he thought, his smile fading as he realized he'd let his guard down too soon again. A bitter taste filled his mouth as he started for Elizabeth's front door. He couldn't help thinking about how things could change so fast.

Resentment welled inside him, and he realized with an unhappy start that some of those good feelings he'd picked up yesterday were disappearing. *Todd did this,* he thought angrily, recalling the look of disdain in Todd's eyes. *All that "good buddy" stuff on the mountain was just another lie,* he decided. Like most of the people he'd known in his life, Todd had turned out to be a total jerk.

He shook his head with disgust as he reached Elizabeth's door. Except for Elizabeth, he realized. Elizabeth had never done anything but care about him. *He* was the one who had screwed up *that* part of his life.

He took a deep breath, trying to still his anger. He had come here to apologize, and that's exactly what he was going to do. Mustering all the calm he could, he walked up to the Wakefields' door and rang the bell.

"It was amazing," Elizabeth told Enid over the phone. She hadn't talked to her best friend since returning from the Great Mountain National Reserve. "I even learned how to catch a fish with my bare hands."

"Great," Enid said, a smile in her voice. "I'm sure that will come in *really* handy the next time we're bored with the menu at the Dairi Burger."

Elizabeth laughed. "It's good to be home."

"Good to have you back, Liz," Enid said.

Just then there was a clicking sound on the phone. "Is that my call waiting or yours?" Elizabeth asked Enid.

"Must be yours," Enid replied. "I don't hear a thing."

"Hold on," Elizabeth said. She clicked the cut-off button. The doorbell rang at the same time. *What is going on?* she wondered. *Maybe Todd forgot something,* she decided. "Just a minute," she told the person on call waiting. She clicked the cut-off button again. "Enid, I'll call you later," she said as she hurried to answer the door.

It was Devon. "I've got a phone call," Elizabeth told him.

"Hello?" she said, picking up the receiver.

"Liz? Thank goodness you haven't left yet!" Jessica exclaimed from the other end of the phone line.

"Did you forget something?" Elizabeth asked her.

"I sure did," Jessica said breathlessly. "I forgot to tell you to take Mom's station wagon instead of the Jeep. The brakes on the Jeep started acting up when you were away, and the mechanic said no one should drive it until he had a chance to check it out next week."

"*What?*" Elizabeth gasped.

"Hey, don't get so worked up, Liz," Jessica said. "The car will be fine. You just can't drive it tonight."

Elizabeth twisted the cord around her hand in a frenzy. "It's not the car I'm worried about," she told Jessica. "Todd went to the deli for me. He took the Jeep!"

"No!" Jessica cried. "Lizzie, you've got to go after him!"

"I'm on my way!" Elizabeth exclaimed, slamming down the receiver and grabbing the keys to her mother's station wagon from a hook on the wall. "I've got to go, Devon," she told him, voice shaking as she ran past him toward the door. "Todd took my car and the brakes are gone. He'll be killed!"

"Wait!" Devon called, racing after her. "We'll take the motorcycle. It'll be a lot faster."

A tight knot formed in Elizabeth's stomach at Devon's suggestion. She and Todd had been in a motorcycle accident a while back. She had been in a coma for three days and had nearly died. Since then Elizabeth had made it a practice to stay as far away from motorcycles as she could.

But Todd was in danger, and she knew that Devon was right—the motorcycle would be *much* faster than her mother's station wagon or even Todd's BMW. They'd be able to zip in and out of traffic if necessary so they could reach Todd before something terrible happened.

Gathering all her courage, she said to Devon, "OK, we'll take the bike. I just hope you have an extra helmet."

"I always carry a spare," Devon told her, leading her to the bike.

Elizabeth and Devon strapped on their helmets, then zoomed off down the street. "Which way?" Devon asked her when they came to the end of Calico Drive. Elizabeth took an instant to think. The deli was on the other side of town, and there were several ways to get there. But Todd had known the deli was about to close. He would have taken the quickest route, over the back roads that led past the beach and into town. Unfortunately the quickest route was also the most dangerous.

"Left, toward the ocean," Elizabeth shouted over the roar of the motorcycle.

Devon took the turn so sharply, they were only inches from the pavement. Elizabeth held Devon tighter. *Devon rode cross-country on this bike,* she told herself. *He knows what he's doing.*

They sped down the winding road, swerving around cars, barely stopping for stop signs as they searched for Todd. "Take a right here!" Elizabeth shouted, pointing to a narrow road on top of the cliffs that bordered Sweet Valley Beach.

Devon roared onto the road, maneuvering

around one hairpin turn after the next until at last they reached a short straightaway.

"Is that your Jeep?" Devon called out, pointing ahead.

Elizabeth glanced around him. About fifty feet ahead of them she saw the Jeep swerving around a sharp curve. "Yes, that's it!" she yelled. "Hurry, Devon! *Please!*"

Devon revved the engine, and they shot toward the Jeep. Even as they raced toward it Elizabeth could see that Todd was out of control, heading toward a cliff. "Todd!" she screamed. But it was too late. As Elizabeth watched in horror the Jeep crashed into a barrier in a shower of sparks and screeching metal.

Chapter 13

Devon heard Elizabeth yell Todd's name above the roar of the motorcycle, and he pushed the bike to its limits. But as fast as the motorcycle was, it wasn't fast enough. Going around a hairpin turn, the Jeep crashed into a barrier before Elizabeth and he reached it.

Elizabeth screamed as the Jeep's right front wheel broke through the steel cable running along the side of the cliff, then slammed into a solid piece of barrier, crumpling it like tinfoil before the steel wedged beneath the Jeep.

Devon's heart leaped to his throat. The barrier had buckled and hooked the Jeep's rear axle. It was all that was keeping the Jeep from plunging to the rocks below.

"Omigod!" Elizabeth exclaimed as the motorcycle screeched to a stop at the site of the accident. "We've got to *do* something!"

Devon and Elizabeth jumped off the bike and

ran to where the Jeep hung precariously over the rocks. Todd was slumped over the wheel, unconscious. The piece of twisted metal keeping the Jeep from falling groaned, ready to snap.

"Todd!" Elizabeth screamed. She reached for the Jeep's front door, but Devon grabbed her arm.

"Don't go near it," he said, holding her back. "That metal barrier is ready to go. One false move and the Jeep will go over with it."

Elizabeth's hands flew to her mouth. "Todd, oh, Todd," she cried, trembling. She looked desperately at Devon. "We can't just *leave* him there," she said, trying to break free of Devon's grasp. "There's no time to call the police!"

Devon held her tightly by her upper arms. "I know that," he told her, trying to keep his voice calm. "And I don't intend to leave him." He looked around quickly, trying to figure out what to do next.

"What are you looking for?" Elizabeth asked frantically as the metal beneath the Jeep groaned again.

Devon let go of Elizabeth and ran a hand nervously through his hair. "I need a boulder or a good-sized log—something heavy to keep the car balanced. Todd's weight is all that's keeping the Jeep from going over. As soon as that weight shifts, the Jeep's going to plunge over the side. It could happen fast, taking Todd and me with it. I'm just trying to give us a better chance."

He glanced around with a sinking feeling. The right side of the road was bordered by the cliff, and the left side was solid rock—no trees, no loose boulders.

Apparently Elizabeth realized this too. "There's nothing like that around here," she said, her forehead deeply furrowed with worry. Then she glanced up at him. "What about if I lean my weight on the Jeep?"

Devon looked at her as if she were crazy. "*You?*" he said. "I don't know if you're strong enough."

"I'm not asking you, Devon," Elizabeth said, obviously annoyed. "I'm telling you. Todd's life is at stake. If anything happens, it's not going to be because I just stood here doing nothing."

At that instant the metal beneath the Jeep creaked and groaned threateningly. The Jeep tilted more precariously to the right.

Devon glanced at the Jeep, then at Elizabeth. "All right," he said. "But if the Jeep starts to go, you jump back, you hear me? Get out of the way."

Elizabeth nodded. "Let's just hurry, all right?"

Devon waited until Elizabeth was at the rear of the Jeep with her hands on the left rear bumper, her legs planted firmly on the ground, leaning forward so most of her weight was on her hands. Then slowly he eased Todd's door open. He grimaced when he saw the deep gash on Todd's forehead. "We're going to get you out of this, Todd," he said.

Even before the words were out of his mouth, the Jeep shifted, and Devon inhaled sharply, whipping his head around to look at the rear of the car.

"It's all right!" Elizabeth called, her voice tense but steady.

Devon let out his breath, then carefully reached for Todd's limp body. Once his arms were around Todd's waist, he called back, "I'm going to pull him out now, Liz. Remember what I told you to do if the Jeep starts to slide."

"Just get Todd out!" Elizabeth yelled.

Devon took a deep breath and pulled Todd toward the road. As soon as Todd's weight shifted, the Jeep began to tilt farther toward the right, pulling the twisted barrier with it. "Move, Elizabeth!" Devon cried, wrenching backward with Todd in his arms. But before Todd's body had cleared the Jeep, it stopped suddenly. Devon pulled harder, but nothing happened. Todd was stuck! Sweat broke out on Devon's forehead. The Jeep was going down, and he couldn't get Todd out!

He glanced desperately past Todd's arms and chest to his hips and legs—still stuck in the car—and saw that a loop of Todd's jeans had caught on the door handle.

"The Jeep's about to go over!" Elizabeth screamed. "Get Todd out of there!"

"I'm trying!" Devon said between his teeth, attempting unsuccessfully to ease the loop off the door handle by moving Todd to the right. As he struggled with the handle the metal barrier beneath the Jeep cracked. Devon knew Todd was a goner if he didn't get him loose—*now*.

Clenching his jaw, Devon yanked Todd with all his might. The belt loop broke, and he and Todd tumbled to the ground just as the barrier broke completely, sending the Jeep smashing into the rocks hundreds of feet below.

Sprawled across the road with Todd's deadweight on top of him, Devon struggled to catch his breath as his adrenaline-induced strength disappeared. He rested on the blacktop a few seconds, then eased himself from beneath Todd, carefully laying Todd's head on the road.

"Todd!" Elizabeth cried, throwing herself over his motionless body.

Devon gently reached down and pulled Elizabeth away. "It's best not to move him or touch him right now," he told her. "He's been pretty badly shaken."

Just then a blue Volvo approached and slowed to a stop. "What happened?" a gray-haired woman asked, jumping from the car.

"There's been a serious accident," Devon told her. "Do you have a cell phone?"

The woman nodded.

"Call the police," Devon said firmly.

The woman nodded crazily. "Yes. Yes, of course," she said, glancing wide-eyed at Todd's crumpled body. "Is he dead?"

"Oh, Devon," Elizabeth cried, burying her head in his shoulder.

Devon held her close to him. He shook his head at the woman, holding his tongue. "He's badly injured," Devon said. "We need help. *Please.*"

"Of course," the woman said, hurrying to her car.

"It'll be all right, Liz," Devon comforted her as they waited for an ambulance. But he wondered how truthful he was being. Todd had been seriously hurt. He'd suffered a severe blow to his skull and maybe internal injuries they didn't know about.

Elizabeth lifted her head, desperately searching Devon's eyes. "Todd can't die," she told him. "I can't live without him."

Devon's heart constricted at her words, but he managed to bite back his own jealousy over the depth of Elizabeth's love for Todd.

"Shhh," Devon comforted, smoothing her hair. "The ambulance is on its way. Todd will be all right." Silently Devon prayed that he would be, even though they'd had their differences and even though he'd obviously lost Elizabeth to Todd. Todd had done so much for Devon in the mountains—and he meant so much to Elizabeth—he just had to be OK.

Elizabeth chewed her bottom lip as the paramedics rushed Todd from the ambulance into the emergency room forty-five minutes later. Hurrying after them, she was pushed to one side by an ER team as they surrounded Todd and wheeled him down the hall out of sight.

"Where are they taking him?" Elizabeth asked the nurse on duty, a young man who appeared to be in his midtwenties with a deep tan and black hair.

"Are you family?" the nurse asked, his hand poised over a computer keyboard.

Elizabeth shook her head. "A very close friend," she told him. "The paramedics said they'd contact his parents."

"Hospital policy is that only the family can be informed of a patient's medical status," the nurse said.

"But I—"

"Only the family," the nurse repeated.

Tears welled in Elizabeth's eyes. *"Please,"* she begged. "I *have* to know. Please help me!"

The nurse glanced uncomfortably at the tears in Elizabeth's eyes. "I'm not supposed to . . . ," he said hesitantly.

A deep sob escaped Elizabeth's throat, and the nurse heaved a sigh. "When the medics called in the accident, they said your friend had some pretty severe head damage. There was lots of blood loss. Possibly some internal injuries. They took him to X ray, and then the doctors are going to do a brain scan."

"A *brain* scan?" Elizabeth repeated in horror.

"I'm afraid so," the nurse answered. "It sounded to me like he's got a pretty bad concussion. They want to know how extensive the damage is."

Elizabeth recalled the motorcycle accident she and Todd had been in, remembered the coma she'd fallen into—total blackness that had luckily lasted only a few days. But some comas, she knew, lasted for years. Even decades.

Another sob broke loose from her throat, and then Devon's arm was around her, leading her to the waiting area. "There's nothing we can do now but hold our breath and hope for the best," he told her.

Elizabeth nodded. Devon was right. All they could do was wait. And she *would* wait, for as long as it took. Even if it took all night.

She wiped her eyes and settled into one of the cushioned chairs in the waiting room, staring emotionlessly at the sitcom playing on the TV across the room. Suddenly a flurry of activity at the entrance drew her attention. The emergency-room door swung open, and in poured Jessica, Lila, Maria, and Winston.

Jessica ran to Elizabeth and threw her arms around her sister. "Oh, Liz!" she cried. "We just heard the news! Is Todd all right?"

Elizabeth squeezed Jessica tightly, then shook her head. "They're not sure yet."

Maria glanced over at Devon, sitting on a corner chair—then at Elizabeth—with a curious look on her face.

"Devon saved Todd's life," Elizabeth explained. "He pulled Todd out of the wreckage."

Lila's eyes widened. "Wow," she said to Devon. "But I thought you and Todd—"

"Todd's been a big help to me," Devon interrupted her. "I'm not saying there wasn't some tension between us, but Todd's one of the few people who tried to make me feel at home in Sweet Valley." He glanced at Elizabeth, then back at the group. "Yesterday Todd helped me out of a serious jam. Pulling him out of the Jeep tonight was the least I could do to repay him," he explained. "And I couldn't have done it without Elizabeth."

"Liz?" Jessica said in a surprised tone of voice, glancing at her twin.

Elizabeth shook her head. "I didn't do anything."

Devon smiled gently at her. "She put her weight on the back of the Jeep so it wouldn't go over the cliff before I got Todd out," he said. "I wouldn't call that not doing anything."

"Neither would I," Jessica agreed, sitting beside Elizabeth. Then she glanced at a team of doctors bustling into a room down the hall, and her forehead wrinkled with worry. "Oh, Liz, I hope he's all right!" she cried suddenly, as if she'd been holding it all in and finally lost it. Tears filled her eyes. "I can't believe I threw this whole party just to cheer the three of you up and you all ended up in the emergency room because of it."

"You threw this party for *us?*" Devon asked incredulously.

Jessica sniffled. "I wanted to make up for what I did. I wanted to help everyone lighten up a little. Instead Todd drove off a cliff because of me."

Elizabeth's heart went out to her sister. Throwing a party wasn't the greatest plan to make up for what she'd done in the past, but Jessica hadn't caused Todd's accident. "Don't worry, Jess. No one blames you," she said.

"You know, I might make fun of you guys for

staying home and watching movies on Saturday nights," Jessica said, struggling to bring herself under control, "but Todd has always been there for me, and I really care about him." She squeezed Elizabeth's fingers. "Even if I *didn't* care for him so much, I love him for the way he loves you."

Elizabeth smiled sadly. "Oh, Jess," she said, squeezing Jessica's hand. "For as long as I've known Todd, I could always count on him to be there when I needed him too." She stared into the distance as the memories flooded back. "Remember that time in grade school when that bully was pushing us around on the playground?" she reminisced. "Todd jumped off the swings and came to our rescue."

"Yeah," Jessica said. "I remember that."

"And how about those silly jokes he used to tell us in middle school?" Elizabeth added gently.

"Todd's been a good friend to all of us," Winston interjected, sitting beside Maria. "He's always had a good heart."

Elizabeth glanced around the room at the small group of friends. *I never even got a chance to tell him I forgave him. Or how much he means to me.*

Elizabeth felt the tears returning to her eyes. *Todd has to be all right—he just has to,* she thought, burying her face in her hands.

"Miss?"

Elizabeth blinked back her tears and glanced up. The male nurse was standing in front of her with a doctor at his side.

"Are you Elizabeth Wakefield?" the doctor asked.

Elizabeth nodded, wiping at her eyes with the scented handkerchief Lila had handed her.

"I'm Doctor Reilly," the doctor told her. "Todd's parents just called us," he explained. "They got the message the paramedics left on their answering machine about Todd's accident and they're on their way. Mrs. Wilkins asked if you were here. She told me she wanted you to take care of Todd for them until they arrive."

"Does that mean he's all right?" Elizabeth asked hopefully.

The doctor nodded. "He's pretty banged up, but in a week or two he'll be just fine," he told her with a smile. "You can go in and see him now if you like."

There was a general cheer from the waiting room, and Elizabeth let out a deep sigh of relief. That's when she noticed Devon sitting by himself, his hands folded between his knees. Their eyes met, and he smiled gently. "Go to him, Liz," he said. "I know your heart belongs to Todd."

Elizabeth looked at him in surprise. *Devon*, telling her to go to *Todd?* It didn't make sense . . . or did it? Devon was a caring, sensitive person. It was one of the reasons she had fallen in love with him. But there were reasons she loved Todd too. Lots of reasons.

She returned Devon's smile, then began to follow the nurse toward Todd's room, where she would tell Todd those reasons—tell him she had made her choice and that she had chosen him.

But as she imagined herself sitting by Todd's bedside, taking care of him until he was well, she suddenly stopped.

When she'd decided to go on the Project Adventure trip, she realized, the whole point had been to choose between Todd and Devon. But suddenly the real lesson she had learned in the wilderness seemed as clear as day. She understood now that the choice she had to make wasn't for Devon or Todd, it was for her*self*. It was time for Elizabeth Wakefield to choose Elizabeth Wakefield, to get to know who she was on her own—without a boyfriend.

Todd didn't need her to sit by his bedside. There were doctors and nurses in the hospital who would take better care of him than she could. And maybe Todd needed time for himself too. Maybe they all did—time to sort things out, to learn to stand on their own.

It didn't mean they couldn't care about one another. It just meant that they had to learn to be happy without depending on someone else to *make* them happy.

She turned back to Devon. "Come with me," she said. "You saved Todd's life. I'm sure he'll want to thank you for that."

The surprised looks on everyone's faces—especially Jessica's and Devon's—was almost comical. Elizabeth stifled a laugh. She didn't want Devon to think she'd been making a bad joke.

"So are you coming?" she asked him, holding out her hand.

Devon nodded. "Yeah," he said. "Yeah, I'd like that."

As she and Devon walked toward Todd's room together Elizabeth felt a great sense of contentment deep inside. She knew she'd made the right decision. To have a complete relationship, she knew now, you had to be complete within yourself first.

She squeezed Devon's hand, and her heart felt as light as air.

"You did *what?*" Jessica shrieked, staring at the words in Elizabeth's diary. She had just gotten home from a *very* successful picnic party. After learning that Todd was all right, she and her friends had returned to Secca Lake to tell everyone the good news. Naturally she hadn't expected Elizabeth to show up. Elizabeth would want to stay with Todd, Jessica reasoned, now that everything was patched up between them.

When Jessica had arrived home, she had been itching to tell Elizabeth what a major success the party had been. That is until now, when she saw what Elizabeth had written in her diary. *That* put the party news to shame.

"What do you mean, you've broken it off with Devon *and* Todd?" she demanded, staring over Elizabeth's shoulder at the neatly written words.

Elizabeth smiled up at Jessica. "Don't you want to tell me how the party went first?" she asked, pulling a strand of grass from Jessica's hair.

Jessica glanced at the grass, and a mysterious smile crossed her face. "Aaron was pointing out the different constellations to me," she replied dreamily. She pulled herself back to the present. "But that's nothing compared to *this!*" she said, jabbing her finger at the diary. "I thought it was *Todd* who hit his head, not *you.*"

Elizabeth grinned. "I know it seems crazy," she said, "but you can't imagine how *good* I feel about this decision." She tucked her feet underneath her. "Look, Jess. I've had a steady boyfriend since . . . *forever!* It's time I learned how to fly on my own—taste freedom for what it really is. How am I supposed to learn who I am if I always see myself reflected in someone else's eyes?"

Jessica stared at Elizabeth in disbelief. Fly on her own? Taste freedom? Had Elizabeth gone *insane?* And who wouldn't want to be reflected in eyes like Devon Whitelaw's? Or Todd's, for that matter. "But Liz," she protested. "They're two of the cutest guys at Sweet Valley High, and you dropped them both—for *no* one!"

Elizabeth laughed. "Tonight it just hit me that I *like* being independent. I like the idea of going where I want when I want with *whomever* I want," she added. She closed her diary and placed it on the nightstand, her eyes searching Jessica's. "I thought you of all people would understand that," she told her twin. "After all, *you* don't like to be tied down."

Jessica sat on the edge of Elizabeth's bed and kicked off her shoes. "But that's *me*, Liz," she said. "I'm a party person, a do-whatever-she-feels-like kind of girl." She pushed her hair out of her eyes and faced Elizabeth. "You, on the other hand, have always had a steady boyfriend. It doesn't even seem like *Liz* without some guy on the other end of the couple line."

Elizabeth nodded, and a knowing smile crept across her face. "Exactly," she said. "People identify me by my boyfriends, not by who *I* am."

"That's not what I meant," Jessica corrected her. "Everyone knows who Liz is, including me. We're twins, for goodness sake. It's just that I always figured a *part* of Liz liked to have one guy in her life at a time."

Elizabeth plumped up her pillow and leaned back against the headboard. "Not anymore," she replied. "From now on, I'm going solo."

Jessica shook her head. "I can't believe you're throwing Devon Whitelaw away," she said. She tapped her chin thoughtfully. "You know, this might just be the aftereffects of being out in the wilderness for a week. I mean, you practically *starved* to death, and who could possibly get a good night's sleep lying on dirt and pine needles?"

Elizabeth smiled tolerantly. "It's not an aftereffect, Jess. I've grown. And part of that growing is I decided I need to be by myself for a while."

Jessica took a deep breath and let it out. "Well,"

she said, pushing herself off the bed, "I suppose if that's what you want to do, that's what you want to do." But inside she was thinking that Elizabeth must be mental. No matter what Elizabeth said, Jessica was sure that the week in the woods had affected her brain. Jessica stifled a yawn. "I've gotta get some sleep. That party really knocked me out."

"Good idea," Elizabeth agreed. "I'm pretty beat myself."

"Good night, then," Jessica said, acting nonchalant. But as she went to her room she was still reeling from what Elizabeth had told her. *Elizabeth without a steady boyfriend? Was that even possible?*

No matter what Elizabeth had said about growing, Jessica knew there was something definitely wrong here. She plopped on her unmade bed and pulled off her stockings, dropping them in a heap at her feet. *Liz will probably be back with Devon or Todd by the end of the week,* she decided. *Once she gets back into her normal routine, she'll realize she needs a boyfriend.*

Jessica nodded to herself, feeling better that this was only a phase Elizabeth was going through. It felt weird having Elizabeth change on her like that all of a sudden.

But as she pulled off her top and skirt, flinging them onto a week's worth of clothes piled on her chair, a horrifying thought popped into her head. What if this *wasn't* just a phase? What if Elizabeth was really serious? *Both* Wakefields playing the field? She recalled how this whole Project Adventure thing had started because Elizabeth had decided to date Devon instead of just staying with Todd. Was it actually possible that Jessica could look forward to losing *more* guys to Elizabeth?

Jessica shuddered at the thought. It was just too terrifying to contemplate. How could she sleep with something like *that* hanging over her head?

Pulling on her robe, Jessica left her bedroom and headed toward the kitchen for a snack. Years of experience had taught her that at times like this, the only thing better than a party was a nice, consoling bowl of cherry-nut ice cream with chocolate syrup. She'd figure out what to do about Elizabeth tomorrow.

It's prom time at Sweet Valley High, and there's only one thing on Jessica's mind—who will be her lucky date? Meanwhile Elizabeth has chosen to stand on her own, but that doesn't do her any good when it's time to find an escort for the biggest night of her life! Will the twins snag their dream men in time for the dance? Find out in Sweet Valley High #141, **A Picture-Perfect Prom?**—*the first book in a magical four-part prom miniseries.*

Bantam Books in the Sweet Valley High series
Ask your bookseller for the books you have missed

#1	DOUBLE LOVE	#51	AGAINST THE ODDS
#2	SECRETS	#52	WHITE LIES
#3	PLAYING WITH FIRE	#53	SECOND CHANCE
#4	POWER PLAY	#54	TWO-BOY WEEKEND
#5	ALL NIGHT LONG	#55	PERFECT SHOT
#6	DANGEROUS LOVE	#56	LOST AT SEA
#7	DEAR SISTER	#57	TEACHER CRUSH
#8	HEARTBREAKER	#58	BROKENHEARTED
#9	RACING HEARTS	#59	IN LOVE AGAIN
#10	WRONG KIND OF GIRL	#60	THAT FATAL NIGHT
#11	TOO GOOD TO BE TRUE	#61	BOY TROUBLE
#12	WHEN LOVE DIES	#62	WHO'S WHO?
#13	KIDNAPPED!	#63	THE NEW ELIZABETH
#14	DECEPTIONS	#64	THE GHOST OF TRICIA
#15	PROMISES		MARTIN
#16	RAGS TO RICHES	#65	TROUBLE AT HOME
#17	LOVE LETTERS	#66	WHO'S TO BLAME?
#18	HEAD OVER HEELS	#67	THE PARENT PLOT
#19	SHOWDOWN	#68	THE LOVE BET
#20	CRASH LANDING!	#69	FRIEND AGAINST FRIEND
#21	RUNAWAY	#70	MS. QUARTERBACK
#22	TOO MUCH IN LOVE	#71	STARRING JESSICA!
#23	SAY GOODBYE	#72	ROCK STAR'S GIRL
#24	MEMORIES	#73	REGINA'S LEGACY
#25	NOWHERE TO RUN	#74	THE PERFECT GIRL
#26	HOSTAGE	#75	AMY'S TRUE LOVE
#27	LOVESTRUCK	#76	MISS TEEN SWEET VALLEY
#28	ALONE IN THE CROWD	#77	CHEATING TO WIN
#29	BITTER RIVALS	#78	THE DATING GAME
#30	JEALOUS LIES	#79	THE LONG-LOST BROTHER
#31	TAKING SIDES	#80	THE GIRL THEY BOTH LOVED
#32	THE NEW JESSICA	#81	ROSA'S LIE
#33	STARTING OVER	#82	KIDNAPPED BY THE CULT!
#34	FORBIDDEN LOVE	#83	STEVEN'S BRIDE
#35	OUT OF CONTROL	#84	THE STOLEN DIARY
#36	LAST CHANCE	#85	SOAP STAR
#37	RUMORS	#86	JESSICA AGAINST BRUCE
#38	LEAVING HOME	#87	MY BEST FRIEND'S
#39	SECRET ADMIRER		BOYFRIEND
#40	ON THE EDGE	#88	LOVE LETTERS FOR SALE
#41	OUTCAST	#89	ELIZABETH BETRAYED
#42	CAUGHT IN THE MIDDLE	#90	DON'T GO HOME WITH JOHN
#43	HARD CHOICES	#91	IN LOVE WITH A PRINCE
#44	PRETENSES	#92	SHE'S NOT WHAT SHE SEEMS
#45	FAMILY SECRETS	#93	STEPSISTERS
#46	DECISIONS	#94	ARE WE IN LOVE?
#47	TROUBLEMAKER	#95	THE MORNING AFTER
#48	SLAM BOOK FEVER	#96	THE ARREST
#49	PLAYING FOR KEEPS	#97	THE VERDICT
#50	OUT OF REACH	#98	THE WEDDING

#99	BEWARE THE BABY-SITTER	#118	COLLEGE WEEKEND
#100	THE EVIL TWIN (MAGNA)	#119	JESSICA'S OLDER GUY
#101	THE BOYFRIEND WAR	#120	IN LOVE WITH THE ENEMY
#102	ALMOST MARRIED	#121	THE HIGH SCHOOL WAR
#103	OPERATION LOVE MATCH	#122	A KISS BEFORE DYING
#104	LOVE AND DEATH IN	#123	ELIZABETH'S RIVAL
	LONDON	#124	MEET ME AT MIDNIGHT
#105	A DATE WITH A WEREWOLF	#125	CAMP KILLER
#106	BEWARE THE WOLFMAN	#126	TALL, DARK, AND DEADLY
	(SUPER THRILLER)	#127	DANCE OF DEATH
#107	JESSICA'S SECRET LOVE	#128	KISS OF A KILLER
#108	LEFT AT THE ALTAR	#129	COVER GIRLS
#109	DOUBLE-CROSSED	#130	MODEL FLIRT
#110	DEATH THREAT	#131	FASHION VICTIM
#111	A DEADLY CHRISTMAS	#132	ONCE UPON A TIME
	(SUPER THRILLER)	#133	TO CATCH A THIEF
#112	JESSICA QUITS THE SQUAD	#134	HAPPILY EVER AFTER
#113	THE POM-POM WARS	#135	LILA'S NEW FLAME
#114	"V" FOR VICTORY	#136	TOO HOT TO HANDLE
#115	THE TREASURE OF DEATH	#137	FIGHT FIRE WITH FIRE
	VALLEY	#138	WHAT JESSICA WANTS . . .
#116	NIGHTMARE IN DEATH	#139	ELIZABETH IS MINE
	VALLEY	#140	PLEASE FORGIVE ME
#117	JESSICA THE GENIUS		

SUPER EDITIONS:
PERFECT SUMMER
SPECIAL CHRISTMAS
SPRING BREAK
MALIBU SUMMER
WINTER CARNIVAL
SPRING FEVER
FALLING FOR LUCAS
JESSICA TAKES MANHATTAN
MYSTERY DATE

SUPER THRILLERS:
DOUBLE JEOPARDY
ON THE RUN
NO PLACE TO HIDE
DEADLY SUMMER
MURDER ON THE LINE
BEWARE THE WOLFMAN
A DEADLY CHRISTMAS
MURDER IN PARADISE
A STRANGER IN THE HOUSE
A KILLER ON BOARD
"R" FOR REVENGE

SUPER STARS:
LILA'S STORY
BRUCE'S STORY
ENID'S STORY
OLIVIA'S STORY
TODD'S STORY

MAGNA EDITIONS:
THE WAKEFIELDS OF
SWEET VALLEY
THE WAKEFIELD LEGACY:
THE UNTOLD STORY
A NIGHT TO REMEMBER
THE EVIL TWIN
ELIZABETH'S SECRET DIARY
JESSICA'S SECRET DIARY
RETURN OF THE EVIL TWIN
ELIZABETH'S SECRET DIARY
VOLUME II
JESSICA'S SECRET DIARY
VOLUME II
THE FOWLERS OF
SWEET VALLEY
THE PATMANS OF
SWEET VALLEY
ELIZABETH'S SECRET DIARY
VOLUME III
JESSICA'S SECRET DIARY
VOLUME III

SVU

Watch out
Sweet Valley
University—
the Wakefield
twins are
on campus!

Jessica and Elizabeth are away
at college, with no parental
supervision! Going to classes
and parties . . . learning about
careers and college guys . . .
they're having the time of their
lives. Join your favorite twins as
they become SVU's favorite coeds!

Look for
the SVU series
wherever
books are
sold.